MW00441327

THE WASP CHILD

BY
RHIANNON RASMUSSEN

THE WASP CHILD

BY

RHIANNON RASMUSSEN

THE WASP CHILD

Copyright 2021 by Rhiannon Rasmussen

All rights reserved

No part of this book may be reproduced in any form or any electronic or mechanical means, including information and retrieval storage systems, without written permission from the author, except for the use of brief quotations in a book review.

Cover art, design, and illustration © 2021 by Rhiannon Rasmussen

Design and interior by ElfElm Publishing

Available as a trade paperback, hardcover, and eBook from Vernacular Books.

ISBN (TPB) 978-1-952283-17-8
ISBN (eBook) 978-1-952283-18-5

Visit us online at VernacularBooks.com

To my mom,
who believed when I did not

the wasp child holds hisself in mid air

CHAPTER ONE

KESH SCRAMBLED BACK TO HIS FEET AND SHIELDED HIS EYES from the glare and dust. He could barely see Rin and Saize silhouetted against the hovercraft's hatch. Although he could pick out the corporate blue of their student uniforms, their faces were obscured by sun and the hover haze. The dust blown up by the exhaust coated his own uniform and pelted his skin, and no matter how he angled his hand, it stung his eyes.

"You can walk home, you disgusting parasite!" Saize shouted down, crouched to ride out the hovercraft's shivering.

He could walk back all hundred kilometers, sure. Kesh had been watching the dashboard from where he'd been shoved in the back, hands duct-taped together, on top of the research equipment and musty old tarps. It'd been a bumpy ride. He had a pretty good idea of how bruised up he'd be tomorrow. There'd been no point in trying to put up a fight. At least they'd taken off the duct tape before shoving him out the door.

Kesh swallowed the dust, smiled, and waved up at them with

the brightest wide-eyed expression he could manage. "Okay! Meet you there, then? How far is it?"

"I told you he wouldn't understand," Rin said, leaning back in the pilot's seat.

"Freak. I can't believe they just let him go to school." Saize's silhouette retreated inside as the hatch sealed shut.

Poor naïve Kesh. Too stupid to understand he'd really been abandoned out in the rainforest to die of exposure.

Kesh considered trying to grab the edge of the hatch as the hovercraft retreated into the air, but it was already way too high up for him to jump. They'd ditched him at last, like they'd been threatening to do every year he'd been in school. All jokes, right? That's what they told the teachers every time he or Aster tried to have something done about it.

Mostly Aster. She'd kept trying long after Kesh had given up.

"See you later!" he yelled, although there was no way they'd hear him through the sealed hatch. But the last thing they'd see was him smiling and waving.

He hoped it haunted them.

Kesh lowered his hand as soon as the hovercraft was out of sight, futilely dusting himself off, and then turned and walked the other way. Maybe he could find a place where no one would ever discover his body. They'd never be *really* sure if he was dead or not. A lurking ghost.

The thought gave him a sick feeling in his throat—not the idea of his own death, but the idea of Aster in the classroom, waiting for news of him. Graduating, wondering if he was somehow still alive. If he had a shot at survival, he should at least try it. For her. Right?

But there was no way he could find his way back to the colony. The least the two bullies could have done was give him a blanket, or a knife, or any kind of survival gear. He supposed he was grateful that Rin had insisted the tape be cut open before they shoved him out. His reward for being cooperative on the way over.

Didn't it get cold out in the rainforest at night? He'd definitely heard that. There were a ton of safety precautions he'd never paid attention to for field trips he hadn't been allowed on. Deeper in the forest, it was warmer—that one he remembered. And there were edible plants. Something about how it was a big deal that humans could digest the local flora.

The local flora was silent, oppressively so. A stiff breeze rustled the needles clustered under his sneakers. It was far from cold—a bit sticky, even.

"I'm not a freak," Kesh said. The crunch of the field needles gave way to the wetter squelch of denser rainforest ground-cover. Not all of the plants were edible. Some were definitely poisonous. Maybe many of them. "I'm not a parasite. I'm not that weird. I do a full rota of chores. I study. So what, my grades are bad. Who cares?"

It seemed like everyone cared. Kesh kept walking. The silence was broken by an animal call. Some kind of bug. Most of the life on the planet was bugs. They lived in swarms and didn't kick people out of their colonies to die.

No, wait. They totally did. The whole class had just watched a video on bug life cycles. That must have been where Rin and Saize got their grand idea. What were they planning on telling the teachers and admins when they got back? That he'd fallen out of the craft?

Aster was going to be the first one who noticed he was gone at all, when she would try to call him this evening for their normal study group.

"I didn't remember anything in biology because I didn't know I was going to be out here. I'm not even allowed out here! I thought I'd graduate, and . . . I don't know! Clean stuff? You don't need a degree to clean stuff." He made a wide hand gesture, sending the plants around him bobbing, then clapped. His voice had silenced the animals, but the clap was muted anyway, and how tiny his own voice sounded among the towering plants and crunch of his footsteps was equally depressing. "Am I going to die? That's not so bad. Everyone dies, right? Everyone dies alone. That's a poem, I think. Isn't it kind of awful to make kids read something like that?"

Kesh imagined himself dead, decomposing under popped sap orbs and desiccated needles, and felt sick. No cremation, no ceremony.

A loud crack echoed to his right. He started. The noise drove the gross image right out of his head, replacing it with the sudden terrifying conviction that he did not want to die. Not here. Not now. Not alone. And definitely not by being eaten.

Loud noises scared away big predators, right? All he had to do was keep talking.

". . . Is anyone there?" Kesh called out. The words squeaked out in a timid voice which he immediately hated.

Another crack. A snap. The noise came from behind one of those tall plants called a tree, after old Earth trees, even though they didn't look anything like those orderly, green poles from videogames. This tree's purple sap orbs, glisteningly ripe, curled up into a dizzying pattern that sheltered whatever moved behind it from Kesh's sight. He could investigate, but that would mean stepping closer.

"Hello? I see you." That was a lie. Kesh moved backward, tensing to run.

A crunch, and a huge, stooping creature stepped out from the brush. Its shell was iridescent, an oily sheen that blended with the plant's luster. With it came an odd, musky scent, sharper than the wet peat of the forest.

Kesh felt his core untense. He waved at the big bug, but slowly, to not startle it.

"Hello! You're a sansik, aren't you?" he called out.

Sansik were the most intelligent native life on the planet. The teacher would always say that with a laugh and follow up with "But now that we're here", or some other rude aside. Sansik weren't hostile, and they didn't seem to mind passive-aggressive comments from the colonists. They even visited the colony a few times a year. He'd seen them on a few of those visits. From a distance. The smell was new.

Maybe they'd help him get back home.

"I'm Kesh. That's my name, Kesh."

The sansik stared at him with large blank eyes, too big for its flat head. It had mandibles. It worked them while it stared at him, unblinking.

Of course it wasn't blinking. Bugs didn't have eyelids.

Behind it, two more sansik lumbered over. Maybe they were laying trails, and that was the smell. Could humans smell it? Probably covered that in class. The first sansik was bigger than the other two by half again, and its head was crowned with spires of chitin. Sansik had some kind of ranking system they grew into. The smaller ones were a kind of foraging drone, and the bigger one with the crown was . . .

. . . Just like on a test, the information didn't come up when he needed it. Royalty, he decided. The bigger ones were usually a sex similar to Earth mammalian female, and crowns meant royalty.

Bigger was subjective. All three were bigger than he was and had an extra pair of limbs folded up against their sides. All three of them chewed their serrated mandibles and stared at him with fractured, shining eyes.

"I'm from Meridian. You know, the weird building full of people like me," he said, putting careful emphasis on each syllable. Friendly. Nonthreatening. No response came. "I'm lost. Can you take me back there?"

The royal sansik looked up, behind him. Kesh glanced around. Just forest. Was that the direction of Meridian? Imagine if he showed back up escorted by sansik. Everyone would be impressed, even Rin and Saize. Maybe they'd even be a little scared. If they were scared, they'd probably just do a better job of killing him next time. Kesh swallowed. "Well, forget about it. I don't want to go back there. It's horrible. You should go away and let me die."

The royal sansik lowered its head to stare at him again. Kesh crossed his arms, burying his shiver deep inside him with the motion, and stared back, unblinking, for as long as he could.

Finally, it stepped back, then turned and crashed through the underbrush. The other two turned to follow.

They really were leaving him.

They would be the last sentient creatures he ever saw.

His knees almost gave out.

"No, no, no, wait! Wait for me, I changed my mind!" His voice cracked. Tears stuck to his cheeks, despite all of the effort he'd put into staying stoic. Staying determined. Cheerful. He gritted his teeth and ran after the retreating bugs.

"Don't leave me!"

All three sansik stopped in their heavy tracks simultaneously. Kesh tripped over the royal sansik's tail and landed face-down on the ground again, jarred out of breath. This time, he sucked in a big lungful of mud. He coughed it out, curled up, and screamed. He hurt. He was ankle-deep in mud. The bug had probably tripped him on purpose.

When he was out of breath, something hard nudged him in the side. He wiped his face slowly. His whole body was sore, face runny and damp. That was just how crying felt.

The royal sansik was leaning over him. The other two boxed him in. Kesh took a deep breath. What should he call the royal one?

"You're uh . . . the queen, right?"

All three stared at him. He tried to remember any of the other lectures or articles on the datapads. The sansik weren't usually violent. A few of them could speak to humans, but apparently not these ones.

The queen leaned closer, luminescent eyes fixed on him, boring directly through him. He could smell its disgusting breath, the same acrid smell as the colony's hospital wing. Kesh always ran his uniform through the washer twice to get rid of that smell.

He took another breath.

"Can I go with you?"

No response.

"I don't have anywhere else to go. If that's okay, I promise I'm not weird or . . . bad or anything. I mean I'm a good person, I'm just bad at tests. But you don't have those, so who cares, right? I can help carry stuff or something. They just dumped me out here like they dumped me everywhere else like it's my fault I'm doing badly! Everyone else gets a second chance, why not me? Aster's the only one who even helps me study!"

His eyes burned with tears. He was babbling. Now they'd

definitely kill him, just to shut him up. The queen sat back, gaze still fixed on him, and then clambered to its feet and turned away. Was it his imagination, or was it walking slower this time?

Kesh rolled over and scrambled after it. *Her*? Did it matter to the sansik? *Her* sounded more queenlike.

He caught up to her, trotted beside her. He had to take three or four steps to measure up to each one of her lumbering strides. "It's okay if I come along, right?"

Her tail coiled slightly, like a scorpion. Kesh tapped her on the arm. Her carapace felt like cold metal. "Okay, I'm going to call you Queenie." He pointed to the bug on the left. "And you're . . ."

The biologists claimed to be able to tell individual sansik apart, even from the same ranks, but to Kesh the two flanking drones looked identical. "Uh . . . you're the queen's guard, like in a game. Hey, where are we going, anyway?"

He could have been talking to Meridian's wall. They couldn't understand him, after all, just tolerate him. Translator was a special sansik rank, and none of these three were one of them. Had anyone been rescued by sansik before? People went missing in the forest, sure. Maybe they were going to pretend to help him, then take him back to the hive and eat him alive.

Yeah, that seemed likely.

He followed the three of them anyway, the queen and her guard, for hours. Long enough for it to get dark and the cold to set in. Long enough for him to count all of the ways the sansik might kill him. Some of the bugs on this planet laid their larvae inside living hosts. Some of those were as big as people. He'd seen pictures in class. Diagrams. And he was being such a nice host, walking back with them so that they could plant their eggs inside his chest cavity. He tried to tell himself the sansik didn't do that, but his mind had already run off in gory detail with the possibilities.

And the air was cold, even through the dust and dried mud caked on Kesh's clothes and face. He was so filthy. He streaked his face with dirt every time he tried to wipe away the tears. He hated being filthy. He'd tripped so many times that he didn't want to keep count. He'd be one giant walking bruise in the morning, if there was a morning.

They walked. They didn't stop to eat or rest. They didn't stop. They walked until his legs shook. Until Kesh's foot twisted under him and he buckled. Even before he hit the ground, he knew this was it: this time he would stay down. The impact, the scratching of the plant needles, it all barely hurt. The mud was a relief.

Why bother getting up? Everyone in Meridian was waiting for him to die. Aster would be free of having to talk to him. The bugs could eat him right here as well as they could anywhere else. Or use him to grow their parasitic offspring, or abandon him here. He deserved it, for being so stupid. For just going along with his kidnappers, hoping they'd hurt him less if he cooperated.

He flinched when claws pulled at his clothes, ready for the tearing, serrated fangs to follow. They didn't. Instead, Queenie scooped her claws under him and cradled him against her chilly shell.

She carried him back to their hive.

CHAPTER TWO

KESH DIDN'T REALIZE HE'D FALLEN ASLEEP UNTIL SOMEONE woke him up by pouring cold, sticky goo all over his face. The sansik were trying to drown him, or the colonists, anyone, did it matter who? He bolted upright, coughing, and found himself sitting in a dim room. The walls glowed in wide, lazily spiraling patterns. Deliberate designs? The luminescent swirls and blooms looked organic enough to have grown naturally.

A bug stood over him, liquid still dripping onto his forehead from the gourd that dangled from its claws. Kesh scrambled backward, his hands sinking into the mossy floor of the room. The sansik's head turned to follow his movement, unhurriedly.

Kesh wiped his face. He could still breathe, although the goo coated his mouth inside and outside and at least some of his cheeks and nose. An oddly familiar sweetness. Something he ate at the colony.

He licked his lips, trying to get as much of the stickiness out of his nose as possible, all too aware of the giant bug watching him.

It was . . . honey?

Kesh wiped his face again, but that just made his hand sticky, too. He grimaced and wrinkled his nose, scouring his memory for how insects made honey.

Honey was vomit.

"Were you trying to wake me up? This isn't . . . uh . . . vomit, or anything, right?"

Kesh covered his nose and mouth and took a deep breath through his teeth, trying not to smell the overwhelming syrupy sweetness while he wanted to retch. The sansik held the gourd out to him.

"Do you have any water?"

It twitched its mandibles and held a claw to its mouth, tipped it up delicately in a pantomime of drinking. Now it was Kesh's turn to stare. The sansik's oily sheen of variegated colors, shimmering over a patterned blue and violet carapace, looked familiar. It nudged the gourd, raised the claw again, and waited.

"Are you Queenie?" he asked carefully, not wanting to offend it. "The one that carried me here?"

It smelled like her. Made sense he'd know how she smelled, since she'd been carrying him. If he got back to school, he had to remember not to tell anyone that. Well, Aster might think that was cool.

Queenie pushed the gourd forward and twitched her mandibles again.

She wasn't trying to kill him. She was trying to feed him. Kesh lifted the gourd and took a small sip. It wasn't so bad. The colony used this honey as a sweetener all the time. They traded with the sansik for it every six months or whatever. A big showy affair. The sansik had never looked super impressed with the ceremonial aspects.

The taste was fine, but the method the honey was made by was another thing. He tried to push the intrusive visual of Queenie regurgitating the goo into the gourd while he crouched in front of her. Her head was as big as his entire chest. Well, that didn't mean much. He'd always been kind of scrawny.

He lowered the gourd to talk, and Queenie loomed in closer. To listen?

"I, uh . . . thanks?"

No response, not that he expected one at this point. Kesh raised the gourd again. It was green, serrated on the bottom, not like any kind of plant he knew of. His thumb sunk into a decidedly fleshy spot. When he tipped it up, a bristly leg stuck out of the other end.

The gourd was the shell of a large beetle.

Kesh made a strangled yelp and dropped it. Queenie tilted her head to regard him with a side-eye that he could only read as disapproving. She scooped the gourd back up and offered it to him again.

He did not want to insult her. She was easily three times his size. He'd heard some of the sansik ate raw iron ore to strengthen their shells. She looked like she could eat raw iron.

Kesh sipped at the honey, gaze nervously locked on Queenie's bright eyes, until she finally moved away out of either satisfaction or disinterest. Either suited Kesh. He set the gourd down and rolled up to his feet. He'd been intending to jump, but he hurt way too much. Honey had dried on his face and down his neck and was matted in his hair and eyebrows and probably his eyelashes. He was gritty, sticky, and gross, but at least he hadn't been eaten alive.

Yet.

Three smaller sansik entered from a passage on the far end

of the room, and Queenie greeted them by bumping heads. They hunched together in an impromptu huddle clicking and wiggling their face-parts on their almond-shaped heads.

What was the standard procedure for unplanned contact with the sansik? Asking for a translator? He must have violated every rule by now. But . . . he was here, so the only one stopping him from getting a second chance this time was himself.

Kesh wrapped his arms around himself and said, as loudly as he could muster, "Do you have a translator I could use?"

The sansik straightened their broad shoulders and turned to look at him as one. They worked their mandibles. Iridescent Queenie stepped forward.

As you called I, Queenie, she said. Her voice grated and issued from her chest, not her throat. It was so harsh and buzzing that he winced.

"Why didn't you talk before?" he asked.

Queenie pressed her head to his. Her glittering eyes did not—could not—look away.

Meridian hive has few larvae and must count them all. Why was Kesh larva abandoned? You are ill?

"No!" His eyes stung, and his fingers were sore. He wiped his face to blot the tears and got honey in his eyes, which burned worse than the tears. "I'm just lost! I'm not ill, or a freak, or weird or abnormal! It's just that my parents are dead and no one wanted to raise me so I just kind of got shuffled around with whoever else had a kid my age, and I'm not very good at school so some of the other kids decided to throw me out because they hate seeing me around. It's not like I don't try. Plenty of people get bad grades and go on to be famous and important!" His voice cracked again. He bit his hand to be sure he wouldn't sob.

Lost larva must be returned, Queenie said.

Her crown poked his scalp. Returned to Meridian. Go back to Meridian, go back to school, go back to normal life, being kicked around from family to family, a friendless loser freak kid who couldn't even taste vinegar without getting violently ill.

Not entirely friendless. Aster would be frantically worried by now. And Rin and Saize couldn't cover up the theft of an entire hovercraft they weren't old enough to legally pilot.

Kesh nodded, bumping his head against Queenie's.

"Yeah," he said. "When do we start back?"

Queenie stood. She turned to the other three sansik, then back to Kesh. Her mandibles twitched.

Tomorrow.

CHAPTER THREE

L EAVING TOMORROW MEANT KESH HAD AN ENTIRE DAY IN the middle of a sansik hive to figure out what to do with himself. He ended up wandering around with no particular goal, being ushered out of rooms until he found a corridor with a cistern of ice-cold water filled by a stream from the low ceiling. He squinted at it until he was sure he didn't see anything tiny swimming in it, smelled it, touched it, and finally tasted it.

It tasted like cold water and soothed his throat.

He gulped down several handfuls, then plunged his head in and scrubbed as much of the honey and mud as he could out of his hair at the cost of the last vestiges of warmth afforded by the grime. Then he huddled in a dry corner, shivering. Queenie returned once with another half-shell, this one full of wriggling maggot-things. It was probably his look of frozen terror that made her remove them.

When Queenie stepped into the corridor for the second time, she told him they were returning to Meridian.

"I thought we were leaving tomorrow? Wait, how long will it take to get back?" Kesh asked. "We have to walk, right? You don't have hovercraft?"

Queenie tilted her head. Her mandibles chewed. That seemed to be what she did while thinking.

Long journey with rest. Two cycles.

"Cycles?"

Sundown to down again.

"Oh, days. Two whole days?" That couldn't be right. He'd only been in the hovercraft for maybe an hour. His legs felt wobbly just considering it. ". . . Okay."

Are you unformed for walking distance? Queenie asked.

"No, I can walk, I just . . . haven't walked that far before."

Queenie moved away without replying. Kesh stared at her wide and spotted back, then with a start realized she meant they were leaving *right now.* He pushed himself to his feet and wobbled after her.

There was a line down her back, marked by two rows of ridges with black patches in the shape of inkblots. Something silvery and membranous peeked through those cracks. Folded wings?

"How come we can't fly?"

Queenie made a terrifying grinding noise and Kesh flinched. "I'm just joking."

That was a miss, or at least she didn't have anything to say to it. She was walking slowly enough for him to keep up, stepping over trenches in the corridors and various roots and leaves. He almost caught his foot in a ditch filled with a goo that looked like mucus but smelled like fresh-cut flowers. After that he put a hand on her leg to steady himself. She didn't seem as cold as when she'd been carrying him.

The corridor widened. Other bugs were joining them, filing

out of the side rooms he'd been blocked from. Kesh moved closer to Queenie, trying to stay out of their way, but hopefully not so close that she would accidentally crush him.

The hospital smell was faint, smothered by the peaty bugs and softer smell of flowers. If that wasn't their smell, then what was it? He had no idea, but after that walk and ice-cold bath, if it could be called a bath, even a stiff old hospital bed sounded good right now. He couldn't wait to get back to his bedroom with real sheets and real pillows and heated by a real heater in a warm flat that wasn't constructed from dirt, beetles, and spit.

He'd said he could walk, but there was no way he could walk for two whole days. Why'd he say that? Bravado? Wanted to seem useful? Why? What was she going to do, leave him after she'd asked if he wanted to be carried or not?

Kesh squeezed up to Queenie's leg and pulled on a fleshy gap where her armor met one of her elbows. She stopped.

"I'm too unformed a larva to walk so far," Kesh said. "I'm tired just from walking down the hall. Can you carry me?"

He held his breath, irrationally waiting for her to say no or rip his head off. That was why he almost screamed when she crouched and scooped him up against her chest all in one motion. He clutched at her claws while she settled him against her carapace. Under-carapace? It felt weird to still call it a chest while the ridges of it dug into his arm. Surely that phrase was too human. The corridor didn't seem so cramped and the other bugs so eager to crush him from up here—he must have been near Queenie's viewpoint.

Several of the drone sansik were carrying out fat little larvae, wiggly grubs with clusters of beady eyes. The grubs were cute in a way, squishy and deformed with big eyes and small chewing mouths. They looked soft to touch, like pillows. Almost like human babies, if you ignored their cleft mandibles, the slight pulsing of their skin and their color, which was reminiscent of white mold. One or two had bright red patches blooming across their backs.

Queenie followed these worker drones up through the tunnel and through a curtain of dangling vines. The tunnel opened to a hall of twisted roots that formed into towering trees overhead. An entry hall of tangled, knotted pillars. Even filtered through the branching roots and the distant high canopy of interlocked branches and pale globes, the daylight made Kesh squint and shade his eyes.

The drones fanned out to the side, ignoring Queenie as she continued down the path. Kesh clung to her shoulder, craning his neck to keep watching as they passed. Beneath the entrance's scaffolding, worker sansik were sorting the larvae into groups. The unmarked larvae were being examined and then placed in front of gourds. The ones with the red spots were being placed on a root, and a sansik of Queenie's size and coloration was killing them. She severed them in half with a wet tear, spilling out crimson across the roots. The color of human blood.

The drones didn't flinch. Queenie didn't look back. The other larvae didn't even seem to notice, suckling on the honey they were given. The queen swiped the parts aside, arms spattered with gore, and picked up another. This one made a high-pitched mewling cry before it died.

A heavy weight settled in Kesh's ribs with the acrid blood-stench. The hospital smell. Sickness and putrefaction.

"What are they doing?" Kesh said. He fought down the cracking in his voice, but it rose despite himself. Could she hear fear in a human voice? If he cried, would she kill him?

He shoved down the panic and focused on breathing. It felt like he waited a year for her to answer, except that they weren't far enough away to mask the scent or sounds of the executions.

Purging parasites, Queenie said. From so close her voice was overwhelming.

"Oh," he said, a harsh exhale of relief as much as a statement. That was right. Another gruesome factoid from biology class. Parasites. Larvae impersonators were part of the life cycle of solitary wasps. Xenobiology had termed them sanguinolent wasps for their vivid color. Not old Earth wasps, but named after them for their parasitic life cycle. Old Earth wasps had stingers. Sanguinolent wasps did not. They didn't need them.

It was easy to imagine that Rin and Saize had dumped him out here hoping that a wasp would find him. Kesh shuddered. Queenie tightened her arms around him, just slightly. Maybe to warm him, or because she thought he was slipping. It was close enough to a hug that he appreciated it either way.

He was glad when they passed into the forest, out of sight and smell of the hive.

The rest of the day they just walked. More sansik joined them as they walked, not just the worker-drones he'd seen before, but other queens—enforcers? Translators? Whatever Queenie was.

Kesh mostly spent the trek nested in Queenie's arms, though he figured out he could tap her and she'd let him down to stretch his legs any time he started to cramp up. Once, after the fifth sansik had joined their little caravan, they stopped by a log to fish out maggots. This time the wriggling reminded Kesh of the struggling, dying larvae, and again he refused them.

Hopefully he'd never be hungry enough to eat live bugs.

Cold crept in again as evening fell. Kesh huddled against Queenie's chest for the light warmth her bulk provided. He shivered so hard it made him sore. His breath puffed white in the air. The chill cut straight through his thin school jacket to his core.

The sansik finally settled down when the light had fully drained from the sky. Whatever invisible signal they'd been following seemed to have been satisfied, and there were five guards alongside him and Queenie. Was that how many usually went to Meridian? Kesh couldn't remember. He'd just been impressed at how big the sansik were in real life.

Queenie was faintly luminescent, blue and yellow swirls tracing her head, shoulders, and back, echoing the patterns in the hive. None of the other sansik shared these patterns. He clung to her arm while she sat, but she didn't shake him off or set him down. Outside of her glow, the forest was pitch-dark, an ominous and rustling quiet. If he squinted, he could see the silhouettes of the other five sansik clustering around Queenie.

Kesh took a breath that burned the inside of his nose and throat and looked up at Queenie. She bent over, pincers gaping, a black-fanged gouge in the night. He pressed himself as flat as possible away from her mouth.

"I'm cold," he mumbled.

She closed her mandibles.

It is the cold season, Queenie said. She closed her claws around him while the other bugs settled in. She smelled comfortable, like pine and moss. He kind of liked the smell. Her lap wasn't warm, exactly, but her body blocked the wind, and all of them huddled together did make a sort of shelter, so eventually he fell into a fitful, shivering sleep.

Queenie woke him at dawn by dumping him unceremoniously off her lap onto the hard ground. Kesh clambered to his feet and took stock of the various now-familiar aches in his body. He was rotating his arm, trying to figure out the difference between a worrying pain and a normal bruising pain, trying to ignore how hungry he felt, when Queenie shoved a claw full of maggots in his face.

He screamed, backpedaled, caught his foot on a root, and landed jarringly on his back. Queenie leaned over him, claw still full of maggots. They were the same color she'd offered him in the hive, but now with bonus purple moss and some clay stuck to them.

Eat, she said. *Your hive eats too little and does not pupate.*

It took him a second to catch his breath.

"What?"

Your hive. Soft. Queenie pushed his arm to demonstrate, he supposed, that he was unshelled. *Wrapped false cocoon. Eat.*

He sat up and dug his hands in his hair, torn between the absurdity of trying to explain to Queenie that humans didn't spin cocoons and only had the one stage, skeletons mostly on the inside, and trying to ignore the squirming things in her hand.

He was shaking. Tears threatened again. Hunger seemed like it was going to gnaw a hole in his gut, and his neck was sore from the awkward angle he'd slept at.

They'd been travelling for a day. That meant he was halfway home. And he did need to eat. Meridian ate these maggot-worms too, just ground into flour, he was pretty sure. There'd been a class tour. No one liked it. Maybe those maggots hadn't been these exact ones but something close. So he could do this. Food was food, wasn't it? Kesh took a deep breath and then grabbed a handful of them.

"Nobody likes me. Everybody hates me," Kesh muttered under his breath, sing-song. The maggots didn't look any more appetizing the longer he stared them down, but their wiggling and twitchy little legs started to bother him less. "Guess I'll eat some worms."

He closed his hand and squished them. Better ooze than wriggling in his mouth. He shut his eyes when he swallowed and pretended it was porridge. It tasted like porridge. Porridge and dirt. The next handful went down easier. If anyone from Meridian could see him, they'd hold him down and—

Kesh covered his mouth and forced down the nausea. No one could see him. No one would know. Actually, if it didn't make him sick, Aster might think it was even kind of interesting. She was weird like that.

Something crashed in the forest. Queenie's head snapped over to look to Kesh's left. He looked up, wiping the worm guts off of his hand onto his filthy pants.

All six of the sansik were staring at a monster the color of spilled blood.

Branches snapped and orbs burst under the weight of the monster's charge, legs moving too fast to count. It had more than four legs. More than the six limbs of the sansik. Kesh forgot about the worms, forgot about school, forgot about being sore and wrenched himself backward, as far behind Queenie as he could get.

The monster was a sanguinolent wasp.

Wasps were a lot bigger than they'd looked in pictures.

Queenie's wings bristled out to each side. She rattled, blurs of bright yellow and blue louder than the generator engines under Meridian. One of the smaller sansik pulled Kesh between its legs and crouched down. He could just see between its arms.

Eerily silent against Queenie's furious buzz, the wasp flung itself at Queenie. Kesh covered his head automatically.

He caught a flash of color and bright clusters of eyes over a gaping maw, a splay of red claws before Queenie struck it across the face.

There was a resounding crack. Fluids sprayed from the gash, spattering Kesh's arms. The wasp snapped backward, and the moment its hind legs touched the ground, it skittered back into the brush. It didn't seem so big now that it was running away. Maybe a third of the size of Queenie. A little bigger than Kesh. Pointier.

Queenie watched it retreat. The breeze dying as her beating wings stilled.

Kesh slowly uncovered his head. A foul, stinging taste in his throat made him gag, and he hastily wiped the spatter of wasp spray off his lips with the back of a dirty hand. Was it poison? He'd never heard of it being poison, but what did he know?

"Are you going to go after it?" he asked as it receded into the distance.

Queenie tilted her head and fixed him in the gaze of her unblinking and slightly luminous eyes.

Meridian is our priority.

". . . Okay."

That was the first time he'd felt like a big deal in a flattering way.

With that, Queenie picked him up, and the bug caravan set out again, in silence. Kesh tried filling the walk with chatter a few times, but when he got one-or-none-word responses he gave up and tried to study the scenery. Practice identifying native plants or something. He was pretty sure he got at least two right. As soon as he was home he could take a hot shower and go to bed. Then the next morning he'd tell Aster about his adventure and everything. Maybe get some days off school.

At last, the trees thinned, and a silver crescent peeked through the needle-trees. The sight of Meridian's dome rising over the forest canopy had never filled him with this much joy. No more maggots, no more giant carnivores. He'd be warm. He'd have clean clothes. The thought of clean clothes reminded him of how gross he must look. Kesh tried to comb his hair out with his fingers. The coarse strands hurt, and there was a big matted patch on one side. Oh well. It'd come out with soap and a comb. And who cared if he looked bad, anyway? He'd survived three days in the forest by himself!

Okay, maybe not entirely by himself. He hoisted himself up onto Queenie's shoulder to look over the procession of Queenie and her five guards. What if he couldn't tell Queenie apart from the rest if he ever saw them again? She had saved his life. After a moment of thought, he scraped through the oily shine of her carapace to create a lopsided Q in her shoulder.

No sooner had he finished than a pain twinged through his fingers. He pushed on the tips. His pointer fingernail felt loose.

Had he torn it somehow when he fell? Kesh pressed harder, and the fingernail came out. Just peeled out from the finger, gone. Clear liquid oozed from the cuticles and the raw skin under it. But there was no blood. Kesh bit his lip to keep from screaming and closed his hand into a fist. It was okay. He was fine. It was just one fingernail, and those grew back.

He checked his other hand. His right pinkie was also raw. What if it wasn't from falling? What if it was a horrible alien fungus on the forest floor and he was poisoned and dying? Or some kind of reaction to what he'd eaten. Allergic? He'd had sansik honey before and never reacted like this.

The maggots. It had to be the maggots. His feet hurt too, but he'd have to take off his boots to tell if the toenails were also falling out, or if it was just from sleeping in them. And all the walking.

Queenie stopped ten meters away from Meridian's silver perimeter wall.

This is your colony. Call your begetters out to greet us.

"You need to let me down so I can go over to the airlock doors. There's a control panel."

Queenie's arms tightened so he could not climb down.

Properly they will come out to meet us.

"But I have to open the—"

One of the panels crackled awake. "Kesh Ugomi!"

Kesh cringed. The whole colony must have heard that harsh blast of noise.

It crackled again. "We're assembling a team to retrieve you."

"We want to talk to someone," Kesh shouted.

No answer. It occurred to him maybe he should have asked for someone specific. Did Meridian have a head diplomat?

After a long enough time for his legs to cramp up again, the airlock dilated and six people emerged, each clad in freshly-pressed official-blue uniforms. The fancy uniforms, worn for board meetings and the Founding Day festival. Four were security guards he vaguely recognized but didn't really know, in masks and armed. The other two were Dr. Shima, a tall and pale man, and Erika Vandelier, chief exeuctive of Meridian and Saize's mother.

Queenie extended her wings. At the sight of the weapons? Kesh tensed.

We have returned your Kesh Ugomi larva, Queenie said. *Polite colony will show favor for such an act, or larva will choose to stay with the group that acts with propriety.*

Choose to stay?

No! No way, he was so close. He wanted to go home!

Kesh tried not to cry or wriggle like the doomed red-spotted larvae. The sansik were holding him hostage. Why did her words gut him? Why did he feel so betrayed? He should have known the sansik would have let him die out in the forest if they hadn't wanted something.

"What do you want?" Vandelier asked. She looked tired. Probably because her child was a societal menace.

Eighteen cycles of advice from your knowledge bearers. There is fungus in the pinewheat. Assistance benefits all hives.

"We can't spare the personnel right now." Vandelier shifted her stance and nodded at the guards, who adjusted the pistols at their belts like they were expecting a fight. "We've also been dealing with the shortage. We've had to cut down on field research."

Without an offer, the bugs weren't going to let him go. Kesh discovered a gap between Queenie's arms. He eased down through it, but before he could take even one step toward Vandelier, Queenie caught a claw on his collar and yanked him to a halt.

Two boxes of fertilizer and the metal cart to pull them in. One box of pinewheat seed.

His heart was pounding so hard it echoed in his head. Did the colony even consider him worth that much?

"We can't spare the seed," Vandelier said.

Of course he wasn't.

Queenie made that earsplitting grating noise again. Kesh covered his ears. Dr. Shima winced. Chief Executive Vandelier was unmoved.

Queenie bowed her head. After a moment of silence, she spoke again. *The fertilizer and one cart.*

"That's fine," Vandelier said. She turned to the security escort, who relaxed. "It's approved. Call it in."

Queenie held Kesh by her side until crates were hauled out through the airlock. Her guards pried the lids off and sorted through them with their three-fingered claw-hands until they were satisfied. They dragged the boxes away, behind Queenie, and then she released him. He ran over to Vandelier as the bugs turned and walked away, back into the forest without so much as a goodbye.

A bargaining chip. That was the only reason the bugs had saved him.

"You look awful," Dr. Shima said with a frown and a shake of his head. "What are those fluids on your face?"

The thought of the story he had to tell perked Kesh back up a bit. "It's wasp blood! Queenie just slapped it—"

"Shit," breathed Vandelier, taking several hasty hopping steps back like he had sprouted slimy poisonous tentacles. "Don't come any closer."

Shima also backed away as he gestured to the guards. "Call in medical decon for a hazmat intake. Kesh, wait at the airlock until we tell you to come inside. Stand here. Do *not* run away again. You might have been poisoned."

All of his words, thankful and otherwise, dried up and lodged in his chest. All except one.

Poison.

CHAPTER FOUR

KESH STOOD ALONE, SHIVERING IN THE WIND, FOR AN ETER-nity. Was that what Saize and Rin had told the adults? That he'd run away? Maybe they hadn't said anything and pretended they knew nothing about his disappearance.

Maybe no one had noticed he was gone until the sansik brought him back.

When the airlock finally opened, two people in full-body hazard suits that crinkled when they moved stared back at him through clear face masks. They indicated he should get onto a cargo trolley, which had been kitted out with a big rectangular plastic bag. Once inside, the tiny enclosed space weirdly reminded him of the sansik grub cells. They sealed him in and then scoured the airlock and the ground outside with a hazmat blast.

"Why are you doing this?" he asked when they came back in. He was still shivering, but not from the cold.

"Standard procedure," said one of the techs.

"Yeah," muttered the other one, "standard lies."

"Lies about what?"

The two exchanged looks. When their mouths moved behind the face masks, he realized they had switched to talking about him over their radios so he couldn't hear. He couldn't shake the horrified looks Vandelier and Shima had given him, the way they'd skittered away. He scratched at the dried fluid at his cheek with a middle finger, and the nail began to work loose. Another one? He tried to remember if the first nail had fallen off before or after the wasp attack.

"Sorry about this, kid," said the second tech.

"Hold on to the rail," said the first.

They hauled him, sitting on the trolley, to the back wing of the hospital where they put people who had contracted sicknesses out in the wild forest. The quarantine suite had a small decontamination room with a rolling steel table, multiple spigots and hoses, and a shower drain in the floor.

Two nurses wearing hazmat suits stripped off his clothes and watched as he showered down with water first and then with a shower of detergent-laced water that smelled gross. It was humiliating, but at least they didn't talk to each other through their radios as if they were commenting on him where he couldn't hear. They didn't say anything at all except to tell him when to wash one final time with ordinary soap.

He lost more nails in the shower. They collected by the drain, along with his own shed hair as he scrubbed and scrubbed. The water was hot and soothed the tense muscles in his neck. He even got the matted patches out of his hair. It wasn't as satisfying as it had been in his imagination.

When he was clean, he put on a hospital gown and was led through a door into an exam room with a bed and monitors. The nurses asked him simple questions and ran tests, weighed him, X-rayed him. Did they do this for everyone who got lost? Probably. Who knew what people could die of out there? Allergic reactions. Alien diseases. Poison.

He stopped paying attention until Dr. Shima came in.

"How are you feeling?" The doctor's voice sounded tinny through the hazmat suit's speaker.

"Tired," Kesh said. The room was empty except for the monitoring equipment and a poster that listed basic symptoms of ordinary communicable diseases like influenza and coronavirus. Headaches, fever. Hurting everywhere. Fatigue. He had three of those for sure. Hair and fingernails falling out weren't listed. "Am I allergic to the sansik food?"

"Did you look at the X-rays?" Dr. Shima took hold of Kesh's hand with his gloved one and held it up in front of Kesh's face.

All of his fingernails had fallen out. The tips of his fingers were oozing blood like a needle had punctured them from the inside. Something very white was just visible beneath the flesh of the finger whose nail had been the first to fall out.

Bone? He looked away.

"No, I didn't," Kesh said. "Am I allergic to sansik food?"

"Your bone structure," the doctor began.

Kesh yanked his hand away. "What does my bone structure have to do with anything? You should be looking for a parasite or something that got inside me. Fungus can make your fingernails fall out, right? It really hurts."

He bit his lip to stop the babble.

"You could say it's a parasite," Dr. Shima agreed. Through the hazmat face plate, his expression looked bland, like he was bracing himself for a loud sound so that it wouldn't startle him when it came. "I can give you painkillers, but I can't help you with the, ah . . . changes."

"What changes? Did I catch a disease? Can sansik food or . . . or wasp blood poison you?" He wouldn't cry.

The doctor reached for Kesh's hand again, but he scooted back to stay out of his reach. "As far as I can tell, Kesh, you are having growing pains. We haven't figured out what triggered them. Maybe the wasp blood. That's possible but awfully fast acting. Maybe it was something you ingested at the hive, like you said. What did you eat while you were with the sansik?"

"Growing pains?"

The doctor paused.

He blinked.

He sighed.

Then he addressed the poster to the left of Kesh's head. "There's a period of rapid growth in the third stage in the life cycle of the sanguinolent wasp."

Kesh swallowed. His eyesight blurred until the doctor was indistinguishable from the wall except by movement. When he could finally speak, his voice was cramped and small, but all of his thoughts came out in a muddled rush.

"I have a wasp in me? A wasp egg? Am I going to die? Are there eggs in the wasp blood? That doesn't sound right. Did it happen while I was asleep outside? Wouldn't I have noticed or felt something?"

"Not in you." The doctor sat back. He smelled acrid.

There was a long pause before Shima spoke again.

A long, long pause.

"You were born a sanguinolent."

"That's not funny," Kesh said.

That was what Saize and Rin had called him before they shoved him out the hovercraft door. He'd forgotten. Parasite. Freak.

Shima sighed.

"You seriously expect me to believe I'm a parasite wasp?"

"Parasitoid," the doctor said. "By definition, parasites don't kill their hosts."

Kesh's chest was so tight he could barely breathe, let alone speak, but he managed to force out words, and once they started they didn't stop.

"Why would you say that?! I have hands and arms and no wings or antennae and I'm not poisonous or ten-legged or anything bug-like! What did I ever do to you or anyone?"

A surge of vicious rage swelled up like wings unfolding in his chest. He raised a hand angrily, and when Shima shoved his own chair back, looking startled, Kesh realized he'd been about to hit the doctor. He settled on wiping the tears out of his eyes. The last thing he wanted to do was give the adults an excuse to try to kill him like Saize and Rin had.

"You are poisonous, in a way," Shima said. "Do you remember Dr. Barendt telling you about your condition?"

"She said I had some kind of allergic condition and what I can eat and can't eat, but she didn't say I wasn't human!"

"This is your condition."

"Why do I look human, then?!"

"You're human-born." The doctor got up and fumbled with the video controls of one of the monitors. "We documented your birth."

Shima brought a picture of an older man onto the video screen. Kesh recognized him, although it was a different picture than the one Kesh kept in a small black frame in his bedroom at home. He'd seen pictures of his father as a child, too. The resemblance to Kesh was striking. Everyone said so. Kesh had never met him, because he'd died when Kesh was too young to remember.

"That's my dad." He dug his fingers into the padded edge of the examination bed. The pain distracted him from his rising panic.

"The host you grew in," Shima said. "There seem to be many genetic similarities."

"No," Kesh said. "No. He's my father. My *normal* father."

"Who's your mother, then?" Maybe Shima was trying to sound gentle, but he just sounded annoyed.

"It's not my fault I never knew her!"

The screen changed to show the inside of one of the quarantine rooms, the one with the big drain in the floor where he'd showered. His father was in a surgical gown, lying on a metal table. His eyes were closed. He looked swollen and flushed. A respirator covered his mouth. It didn't look like it was being used. Kesh covered his eyes as scalpels flashed under the bright lights, as blades cut into the patient's distended abdomen.

"I'm not looking at that! You can't make me watch it, it's not true, I don't know why you would have a video like that! What's wrong with you?!"

The video went on. The surgeons discussed parasitoids and nutrients and cavities, and occasionally there were disgusting noises of chewing and swallowing that he didn't want to think about. At least there wasn't any screaming in the video. All the screaming at this moment came directly from him.

"I was born like a normal person because I am a normal person! My dad died in a field accident. I didn't kill him. I wasn't born out of him. That's not why I look like him. Even if I did, I didn't eat him. I didn't because that's impossible and it's not funny so why are you showing me all of this? You're sick. You're all liars and I hate you all, I hate you. That's not how I was born!"

He looked up when there was a moment of silence, hoping the screen was blank, but instead the camera had focused on a half-formed thing with wide black eyes and fat baby limbs covered in blood and smeared with viscera. It made high-pitched repetitive clicking noises. Crying, just like the mimic wasp larvae in the hive. He didn't want to think about the sheet-covered, out-of-focus form behind it.

"That's not me," Kesh said. "That's not my fault. It's not me. Why won't you just shut it off?"

He curled up and hid his head from the light, dug his fingers into what was left of his hair. *Oh god*, he began crying uncontrollably, like his whole body was going to shake apart. He wanted to hurt everyone in the colony for lying to him, letting him suffer, trying to get rid of him over and over again and now trying to pretend that he was a monster and that the problem was with him. Born wrong. Freak. Parasite.

He barely felt the bite of the needle in his shoulder.

It brought respite.

CHAPTER FIVE

K**ESH WOKE IN A NUMB HAZE TO ANOTHER DIM ROOM. A** blanket blotched with a big dark stain covered him from the chest down. Some kind of wet ooze smeared the inside of his mouth. It tasted the way Queenie had smelled when he'd stumbled across her.

Wasp hunting.

She'd been wasp hunting. That was dead wasp musk he'd smelled. When he tried to wipe the ooze off his lips, he saw a translucent spur pushing its way through his fingertip. All his fingertips were tearing open as spurs shoved through the skin from inside. He didn't have to look at his toes to know they'd be the same. That wasn't ooze in his mouth. It was blood.

When he moved, he felt other tears in his flesh: a dull pain in his abdomen, twin sticky, stinging lines like gashes on his back. The change was happening to him everywhere. At least the sansik didn't lie to their larvae. They just killed the bad ones.

Hot bile burned up his throat, his stomach churning with nausea. He held a hand over his mouth until he could breathe without wanting to vomit. It took him a few minutes more to realize the dark patch on the blanket was the shadow cast by Dr. Shima. He'd been standing there like a creep the whole time, watching Kesh wake up.

"Can you hear me?" the doctor asked.

Kesh squinted up at him, at his pale face and hair. "Why aren't you wearing a hazmat suit?"

"We've determined you are no longer carrying anything deadly. Which means you're no longer a danger to us . . ." He hesitated, as if he wasn't sure.

Kesh wanted to not be a danger, so they wouldn't try to kill him. He wanted to give the doctor the stupid vapid smile he'd gotten so good at during class, but he just couldn't.

"It hurts," he muttered instead.

"What exactly hurts?" Shima's eyes crinkled up at the sides, and he had a faint smile on his wide mouth like Kesh was a fascinating anomaly he was privileged to observe.

"Everything hurts."

"We'll continue to give you painkillers for another few weeks as you work through this." Shima sat next to Kesh, picked up his left hand, and examined it. Although he was no longer wearing the hazmat suit, he was wearing blue nitrile gloves. "You've mostly stopped bleeding. A nurse will be in to help you clean up."

Kesh nodded. Stopped bleeding. That sounded good.

"Don't pick at any of the dressings."

"Dressings?"

"Heal-skin. They're for your own protection. The nurses will take care of all that."

"When will I be better?" But the instant he spoke an anxious pressure squeezed his chest. He wasn't human. He would never be better.

"Well, you're an anomaly, Kesh, so we don't know when or how."

Or *if*, but the doctor had the grace to not say that out loud.

"We have to take it one day at a time and keep you under observation. Unfortunately, you don't get a choice in what happens now. Your job is to be patient and let us do our work and take care of you."

"Could you tell my friends Rin and Saize something for me?"

"Sure." Except *I thought you didn't have any friends* was what the look on the doctor's face said.

"Tell them 'Screw you and I hope a wasp rips you to pieces and eats you, or maybe I'll rip you to pieces when I get the chance,'" Kesh muttered.

Shima sat forward. His uniform wrinkled at the shoulders, like it didn't quite fit right. "What was that?"

"Never mind. Nothing. Tell Aster I'm okay."

Shima frowned. "Aster Tiu?"

"Yeah."

"What about Rin and Saize?"

"Just Aster, please." Did he have to spell out that Rin and Saize weren't actually his friends?

"Okay." Shima slapped his hands on his knees and stood up. "You'll have to remain isolated as we keep you under observation. Don't expect visitors."

"What about Aster?"

"What about her now?" Irritation was leaking into the doctor's voice.

"Can she visit me?"

"No. No one except medical personnel can visit you until this is under control."

CHAPTER SIX

I T TOOK A WEEK FOR KESH TO REALIZE THAT THE DOCTOR
meant exactly what he'd said. No one but the medical team came
in to see him. There were monitors on him and one screen he
could turn on and off to watch pre-scheduled programming and
another button he could push to summon a nurse. That was it.

His most recent set of foster parents were technically medical personnel, and they came to visit exactly once. At first Kesh
was thrilled to see them, but in the space of minutes the weight
of their insipid conversation became unbearable. He'd never
thought much about how they were researchers too. Most of the
colony personnel were researchers in one way or another. That's
why people moved all the way out to Meridian.

His so-called parents talked to Dr. Shima as if they were
old friends. Of course they were old friends. Of course they'd
known. They'd been part of the study team, raising him to find
out what would happen. Telling him the standard lies. He was
just an experiment to them, wasn't he?

They left in a hurry when he broke down and screamed accusations at them.

Later, sitting in the bed in his room alone, he felt ashamed, thinking about the things he'd shouted. He composed apologies in his head for when they returned, but they didn't come back and didn't send any messages. Had he been that bad of a son? He tried to remember what they'd done together as a family, but mostly he remembered the routine of colony chores: cleaning, de-clogging, pest patrol, kitchen duty, hauling and stacking bio-solids bricks for the masons. He'd worked the rota alongside his foster parents from as early as he could recall, although they'd never talked much in the way he heard other families chattering. He was quiet. They were quiet. It wasn't wrong to be quiet, was it?

He remembered going to and from school, walking by himself through the main concourse of Meridian to go to classes or sitting in the academy wing corridor alone for noncompliance or for inattentiveness or for lunch since no one would sit with him in the cafeteria. The colorless hallway had smelled of old food and bleach, just like the hospital wing did. A place to be sick and alone. So he'd sat alone and flipped aimlessly through games on the school-provided touchpad.

Aster had been the one who approached him. He'd just started lower second form and didn't remember seeing her in first form. She'd asked what he was playing, so he'd showed her. After that, they would sit together in the hallway. It turned out it made a difference, to be alone alone, or alone together.

As days passed, color bloomed across his skin like a vivid bruise. Not normal colors; these were crimson and a deep blue-black that spread across his body like Rorschach blots. Kesh daydreamed about pricking himself and letting the horrible colors bleed out over the bed and floor until he was human again and a nurse would come and mop him up and give him normal clothes and let him go outside.

But of course that wasn't how it worked.

As the growing pains eased, he was allowed to walk on the treadmill. When he wasn't on the treadmill, or being tested and poked and prodded, or sleeping, he flipped aimlessly through the games on the touchpad, the only piece of equipment he was allowed that wasn't bolted to something. It was one of the pads provided at school, with limited services. Curated offerings. Mostly boring.

Bone spurs—as Dr. Shima called them—slowly replaced his fingernails. They bled whenever the scabs ripped. They caught on everything. They tapped uselessly against touchscreens, and he could barely hold a stylus. All the twitch games he'd been so good at—the only thing he'd been good at—were painful to play. He got worse scores than a five-year-old.

He tried watching dramas to pass the time but found himself jealous of normal lives and petty fights. At least the characters cared enough to fight. They were fake, and their fake problems made him want to scream and throw the pad to the ground and stomp it into pieces. It made him sob, with his cracking face that made snot and slime but not tears.

Aster didn't even send a note. And he thought he'd had a friend. How stupid of him.

The medical team came by once a day to examine him. Their clamor and rustling and questions to each other and the beeps and clicks of their equipment made him want to crawl out of his skin with discomfort, as if crawling out of his skin wasn't what he was already doing. They documented the changes, scabbing, blood, claws, how his face was splitting open at the mouth to make room for new teeth. Kesh tried not to listen as they listed off other unpleasant details. He tried to hold his breath because of their rank smell. He'd never noticed before how *much* people stank of meat and mold.

On the day they announced they would unwrap the heal-skin that had been protecting his abdomen and torso, he kept his face turned away, staring at a wall as they peeled it off and measured and wiped his skin clean of residue. Finally, they all left except his case nurse, Practitioner Bey. Everyone had some fancy title appended to their nametags.

"Just tell me how you feel, Kesh?"

"How do you think I feel? I feel like a freak you guys are studying the way you study bugs."

"Kesh, if you would just—"

"I just *feel* like being alone."

She glanced toward the opaque wall that he was sure was a one-way viewing window, shook her head slightly, then signed off and went out, taking her rancid meat-mildew smell with her.

The silence was his again.

But he didn't really feel like being alone alone. Saying that to them was just the only thing he had control over.

After a while, curiosity got the better of him. What fresh horror had they unwrapped when they'd taken off the heal-skin? He pulled down the sheet and peeked under his hospital gown.

Why were there three gashes around his hips now? They didn't match up with the lines of his new skin. Was his whole skin going to split off him like an overripe fruit? Wasn't this too much change for one body? How long was it going to go on? Couldn't he die in one explosive burst and get it over with?

The questions gnawed at him until he got up and ran and ran and ran on the treadmill. Eventually he had to sit back on the bed, winded. The whirling questions still pummeled his mind, a racket he couldn't turn off. He needed a distraction.

He scrolled aimlessly back and forth through the short list of solo games available until one he'd glossed over before caught his eye. It was an educational biology game for first, second, and third form, out of date and old fashioned even when he was little, the kind of game no one needed to play anymore but wasn't worth the bother of erasing from the system. He and Aster had sunk months of game time into it after the first project they'd worked on together had gotten blown up in the school's shared building-world and they'd received demerits for picking a fight with the kids who had sabotaged it. Of course it had been Saize and Rin.

Those two would laugh at him now for playing a baby game, but he could pretend he was nine and sitting next to Aster in the corridor if he wanted to.

The game's opening jingle made him wince with the bittersweet sharpness of old memory. He had to wipe away slime leaking from his eyes, careful not to poke himself with his bone spurs. He used a forgotten strip of medical tape to fix the stylus to his hand and tapped through to the human anatomy and medicine section. He imagined someone who wasn't Aster asking him what he'd done in the hospital. *I played hospital*, he'd say, like the whole thing was a joke he was in on.

He and Aster had opened this game for the first time because they'd hoped for a taste of the forbidden gore glimpsed on twitch-game download listings, all the grimy stuff which was age-locked off the school pads. But of course this game was textbook, the least exciting possible way to showcase blood and guts. Loading it back up, he noticed it looked even worse than he remembered: garishly colored models of human organs, and deep in the guts a weird blur, like the program was starting to decay.

But Aster had genuinely liked the game. She was good at everything, as the teachers had soon discovered. She'd blazed through the anatomy courses. The surgery game to her was like twitch games for him: the satisfaction of solving a puzzle. So he'd played the assistant, and after Aster had perfected all of the scenarios, they'd made up ridiculous challenges. He could probably still do the left side of the easiest levels with his eyes closed; Aster had taken the right. Staying coordinated had been the challenge.

The stylus kept slipping. The scabs tore and ached when he tried to tape the stylus to his fingers, not just his palm. The practice-patient died over and over until he quit and went into the settings and found the character creator. He made a new patient, a character who was check-marked as biological sex male, gender male, and he gave it black hair and black eyes and black eyebrows and the same stupid blank expression he saw when he looked in the mirror, except this face didn't have a split red carapace from its eyes down to its chin. Not yet. This thing, this avatar, this patient, which didn't deserve to be called a person, he would turn it inside out.

Everything that he could do wrong to the patient, he did. He threw it rag-doll across the room. He made it dance in a macabrely funny way across the lab equipment. He ripped out its guts, pulled the skin out into distorted flaps, screwed spine braces into the ribs, hacked the liver into pieces through the three holes of a laparoscopy—

—the punctures—

He touched the three healing scars on his abdomen. These weren't part of his transformation. These were the marks of a surgery.

What had the medical team done to him? What had they done without asking? Without even telling him afterward?

Because the patient-avatar was bleeding out, the game beeped with a fake emergency alarm. He dropped the pad on the floor and curled up on the bed as much as he could without the holes feeling like he'd been stabbed through. But he had been stabbed. He's been cut open without permission, without explanation. They didn't even care enough about him to tell him why.

He cried until his face throbbed more than his fingers and his wounds. But even crying got boring, and it wasn't really crying anyway. He wiped the slime off his face. Then he lay there staring at the ceiling. Oblivion wouldn't be so bad, would it? At least then he wouldn't feel anything.

But oblivion didn't want to hang out with him either.

When he couldn't get to sleep, he couldn't stand the ceiling's uncaring metal glare, so he picked the pad back up. The game was still on. The screen berated him for letting the patient die. The patient got more rights than he did.

How long did it take for experiments to die?

He restarted the level and cut open the patient's abdomen, a gash from the ribs down to the groin. As the bleed-out timer popped up and clicked higher, he zoomed in, watching the ways blood drained from the body. Was there a time limit? Was there a difference between a person and a body? Did it matter the kind of organs you had, or the kind of parents, or the kind of face?

For some reason, in close-up, the liver model looked abnormal, like someone had scrawled angry doodles on it. No, someone *had* scribbled on it. Down on the caudate lobe, it looked like actual letters. He angled the image around until it was right side up. Where a piece of the lobe had been snipped, the area had been replaced by a gray screen with words.

Words.

HOPE U PLAY NOT ALLOWED CHAT AST

Kesh was so startled that he shut down the pad in a panic. The doctors might be watching through the viewing window. They'd see the message.

Yet as he crossed his arms over the pad, hugging it against his body as if he could hide it there forever, a hot force welled up inside him. A joy he hadn't allowed himself to hope for warred with loathing in his painfully tight chest. Just breathing felt like winning a battle.

How could he tell her he'd read the message? It wasn't a trap, right? No, it took a smart person like Aster to come up with such a garbage way of contacting someone. Only Aster would remember all those hours in detention in the corridor, playing a game no one else was interested in. The message could have been sitting there for the whole time he'd been in the hospital.

He couldn't figure out how to get into any of the game files with a message for her, so he made a bunch of profiles with whatever trash names he could think of, stellar titles like "bored," "bored 2," "guts," and "surgery friend." When the network cycled through its daily update, he hoped it would update the game too. Hoped no one would notice.

Praying wasn't something his parents had ever done, but the breathlessness squeezing his heart was something like prayer when he loaded the game the next morning.

Aster's scribbles on the liver were gone, but there was a new profile beside the ones he'd made, called "guts12."

It took him a few minutes to remember that the duodenum had the word *twelve* in it, from another language, one nobody here spoke. Sure enough, she'd sliced away a tiny sliver of the first section of the small intestine and embedded a message there.

SO MAD SAIZE RIN ONLY SLAP ON HAND BUT ERASE & WRITE REPLY HOW ARE YOU

An ordinary backspace deleted her message character by character and left room for him to type in the box. He had no idea how she'd managed it, but Aster was brilliant at programming and networks and the whole data sphere of the colony. It's why the teachers loved her, why Dr. Shima wanted to protect her from a worthless person—if he was even a person—like Kesh.

What to say? What to say? He didn't want her to turn away from him in disgust.

NEED HELP THEYR CUTTING ME OPEN

Was that too dramatic?

But what did he have to lose? He was already locked up. He might as well find out the worst about Aster, if she really wanted to be friends with something like him.

SED IM SANGIOLNT WASP PARASIT HAHA GUESS IM FREAK AFTER ALL THEIR NEW EXPERIMNT

Then he played the game for a little while so it wouldn't look suspicious, so there would be a trail of play to follow. By the time he had failed the test on skeletal structure three times, he was sorry he'd sent those stupid words at all because now she would never speak to him again, so he pulled up the hidden screen in the duodenum to delete and write something, anything, better.

She had already replied.

I KNOW. THEYRE SHOWING PICS OF UR TRANSFORM IN CLASS. IM SO MAD I FILED FORMAL PROTEST & GOT DETENTION. REFUSED MY REQUEST TO VISIT.

He stared for a long time at the screen, too stunned to move or think. Is that all he'd ever been to his foster parents, to Dr.

Shima, to all of the adults? Some kind of fruit fly allowed to live as long as he was an interesting experiment? A creature to study? Or was he the bug that had killed their respected and beloved colleague?

Hands shaking, he stabbed at the pad and finally managed a reply.

WYAT THY SAY ABIUT ME

The chime rang at the door: duty nurse incoming. He was smart enough to have a side game on standby, and it only took two jabs to shunt into the biology of cereal, legumes, and oil-seed plants.

The nurse wore a cheerful smile as she halted beside the door, looking Kesh over with the kind of caution anyone would use when entering a room with a nasty killer who might still have a sting. "Seems like you're getting the hang of that pad, Kesh."

He stuck his idiot smile on his cracked, misshapen face. For the first time he realized no one here at the colony could read a normal human expression on him, not anymore. He pitched his voice to match the fake cheer of the nurse's smile.

"Yeah, I got bored of the dramas, so I thought I would try reading something. But this pad is locked to lower-form educational programs. I know I wasn't good at school, but that seems harsh. Ha ha. Maybe I could get access to the data web or something?"

The nurse's eyebrows rose. He'd surprised her. "That's not my call. I'll mention it to Dr. Shima. How about we take your vitals?"

He stuck out an arm obediently. "Don't you have my vitals all the time anyway, through the monitors?"

"Sure, but monitors are no substitute for checking in on you in person."

He wanted to ask sarcastically if he was still considered a person, but Aster's mention of detention made him cautious. "Uh, can I get something different to eat, maybe?" he asked instead, figuring that was safe.

"You're allergic to human food, Kesh. Didn't anyone explain that to you?"

"But I eat human food all the time."

"No, you eat pinewheat and worm flour and sansik honey made into food that we call by Earth food names. Your body rejects Earth food substances."

"But everyone here eats pinewheat and worm flour and sansik honey. Why don't they get sick?"

"You've got a lot of questions today." She gave a sharp sigh, although Kesh wasn't sure who she was mad at. "I'll let Dr. Shima know."

She ran through the scrub part of her duties: swabbing samples from his skin and the inside of his mouth and more samples from the room's surface and the pad, then running the disinfectant over everything. She had a way she did things, always the same each time, and he didn't want to interrupt.

Finally, when she'd placed all the swabs bagged and tagged into the wall slot, she went to the door. "Listen, Kesh, it's not that I don't want to answer your questions. It's that things have gotten complicated. Dr. Shima will talk to you."

The door lock clicked shut behind her.

What if I don't want to talk to Dr. Shima? What about that? he wanted to yell after her. He counted to a hundred, and then to a hundred again, pulse racing until it was impossible to wait any longer, even knowing they were probably watching him. Would they ever get tired of watching him split and ooze and distort and change?

He turned the pad back on. A diagram captioned "The Life Cycle of Cereal Plants" flashed brightly at him, a big circle, the circle of life. He switched back to the medical program. Aster had replied.

THEY SAY UR AN AMAZING TEST CASE FR STUDY + RESEARCH. ITS GROSS. ASK IF U CAN GET VISITORS.

He typed back: ALRADY ASKED THY SED NO. CNN WE KEEP TALKNG HERE BUT NOT TO MUCH SO THY DONT GT SUSPISIOUS

Kesh closed down the game and opened up a drama, letting it play at loud volume while he sat with legs dangling over the edge of the bed and, ignoring the dialogue, thought. He was not going to be their amazing test case, a study subject to shove needles into, cut open, and swab until they got tired of him or mad at him and decided to purge him by putting him down.

He had to get out of the hospital, and that meant out of the settlement. Surely the sansik would take him, and not kill him, if he could prove he was useful to their hive. That would probably outweigh the sin of being a wasp, right? So how could he be useful to them? What had Queenie wanted from the colony?

There is a blight in the pinewheat, she'd said. She had told Vandelier that assistance would benefit both colonies, but the executive hadn't listened. Hadn't wanted to help. Not in exchange for Kesh, anyway.

The lock clicked, the door opened, and Dr. Shima entered the room, pulling on blue sterile gloves with his usual nice-doctor expression on his lying face. "Good afternoon, Kesh. You wanted to talk to me?"

"I want to go back to school. I thought I might study agriculture. I, uh, want to do better in school, to help the colony."

The doctor's fake little smile died on his face. "What did the sansik show you?"

"The sansik?" Kesh blinked several times, hoping he looked clueless and innocent and slow. "We saw a lot of dirt and scrub walking all the way here. It was a long way. My feet got sore. I mean, when I still had ordinary feet. Ha ha."

Was he being too inane? Too obvious?

"I'm feeling better. Now I'm bored. I just thought studying and having a job to do like everyone else would be what you all wanted. So I can contribute like everyone else."

Dr. Shima gave him an odd, sidelong look. "I see. I'm afraid your studies will have to be postponed until you're stronger."

"Stronger?"

"The primary molt has taken a lot out of you. We'll discuss your options when you've stabilized."

"Oh. What kind of options?" Primary? Did they expect another molt?

"To be more clear, there aren't options in your development, just unknowns. What's happening now is irreversible."

Irreversible. "Yeah, I figured that out."

"Listen, Kesh, it's only fair we be truthful with you. We don't know whether to expect a secondary molt or how it might unfold in your physiology or your . . . brain."

"Nothing's wrong with my brain!" Kesh shouted, sitting up so sharply that Shima skittered back as if expecting an attack. The door clicked, opened, and a security guard holding a gun stepped in.

Dr. Shima raised both hands, palms out, in a calming gesture. He tried on a grin, but all those rigid teeth just reminded Kesh of skulls and death. "Of course there isn't. But you're unique, Kesh. Nothing like you has ever happened before that we know of. Earth is going to be very, very interested in you. Would you like that? To go to Earth? Not many people who live here will ever get that chance. You're lucky."

Lucky? How could Shima even say that with a straight face? But Kesh had a lot of practice using a blank expression, even with a guard holding a weapon in case his murderous wasp instincts got the better of him and made him attack them. He didn't feel like attacking anything. He just wanted to run away.

"Earth? Really?" he said in a voice he hoped sounded chipper, given the grating grind that underlay all his words now. Just like Queenie. "What would I do on Earth? Can I go to school there?"

The security guard made a little sound, like a grunt of laughter or of disgust. His scent changed, too, and so had Shima's. Kesh was beginning to be able to differentiate between their hormones. Didn't people shed hormones when they had emotions? Aster would know. Shima smelled sour, and the guard smelled like battery acid. It was so weird to be able to distinguish between those smells that Kesh was distracted from Shima's final comments, made in a soothing tone before he left with the guard, who locked the door behind them.

He raised his arm to his head, sniffed at himself. He smelled sweet, like nectar. The sansik had that nectar scent too, but they also smelled like crushed pine. Mossy. He thought it had been so unpleasant, but it was soothingly familiar now. The sansik had a similar fragrance because they were born of this planet. As he was.

The room was silent except for the *tick-tick-tick* and occasional beep from the monitors. Dr. Shima's words cycled back through his mind.

To go to Earth?

Like they would give him a choice. "There were no options," Shima had said. He would either die here and get shipped back in a frozen slab, or he'd be shipped there alive for the scientists on Earth to study. Once he was on Earth, where he couldn't eat the food, he'd never be able to make any decisions for himself, to escape, or to live as anything but a bug in a lab.

When was the next ship coming from Earth?

His only chance to live a life on his own terms was to get out of the colony before the ship got here.

CHAPTER SEVEN

THE NEXT DAY DR. SHIMA ENTERED WITH A BRIGHTER AND cheerier smile than usual. "Good news, Kesh. We believe your primary molt has stabilized enough we can do a new round of tests to see where you're at."

Kesh imagined the insect-baby's unblinking dark eyes on his own face and drew the blanket up to his neck. "Like what?"

"A full-body scan, a few other things. This is good for you."

"Is there going to be a secondary molt?"

"Well, I guess we'll find out, won't we?" Shima was peppy today, almost giddy as he went on. "There's a drone shipment leaving next week for Zenith Colonia. We'll put all your information on it. People are going to be excited about you, Kesh."

Like he had a say in this.

They gave him injections that made him sleepy, put him in a tube and under lights. Machinery whirred at him for hours before they finally put him back in bed.

He woke groggy the next day, hunger and thirst like heat in his stomach that sent him into half-waking dreams of running and hunting and killing. Wasp dreams.

Then the door opened. The day nurse brought him a meal of imitation Earth food, pinewheat and worm flour boiled into fake dumplings and baked into fake bread. His mouth hurt so much from chewing the dense bread that he was afraid the tests had triggered that secondary molt and his skull was deforming even more. But when he felt his head, it was the same as before the tests, a mostly human shape with a pointier top. Not top. Cranium. A pointier cranium and a slightly longer mandible. No wonder the scientists were excited. They didn't understand how sanguinolent wasps did what they did. And here he was, laid out on a platter for their fine dining.

Back when he'd been allowed to sit for supper in the main cafeteria with his foster parents and everyone else, the adults would always be talking about getting a better aggregation score for Meridian Colony. A higher score would mean more resources sent in by the company and more chances for colony kids to get a placement at one of the company universities on one of the major colony worlds, not a low-ranking research base like this one. Bright kids like Aster, who deserved a chance to excel.

He needed Aster's help.

During the tests his bone spurs had been fitted with thin ceramic caps, probably as a safety measure, but the stubs made it easier for him to hold utensils and, most importantly, a stylus.

NEED 2 STUDI AGRICULTRE, he wrote on the duodenum.

OK, she replied. GIVE ME AT LEAST 5 DAYS THEN ASK SHIMA FOR 4TH FORM CURRICULUM. U FLUNKED THAT REMEMBER?

Yeah. Fourth form was when Kesh had really started tuning out, as the other kids rocketed through puberty while he stayed stubbornly childlike, just growing a little taller year by year. That's when the "freak" and "parasite" teasing worsened. That's when he stopped fighting back, because fighting back got him and then even Aster in trouble.

But you didn't have to fight to get your way.

He became the model patient. Rise and shine. Eat breakfast. Walk on the treadmill and, as he got stronger, jog. In ten days he worked through all the first-, second-, and third-form tests on the pad and showed his passing scores to Dr. Shima. He wasn't sure how the scores measured up to other students', but they were definitely his best.

"It's really boring being stuck in here. Can I have visitors besides the medical people?"

The doctor's sour smell spiked with a more acidic fragrance. His lips turned down. "We talked about this, Kesh."

"Can I get the fourth-form curriculum, at least? All I have now is little kid games and dumb dramas. I'm so bored, Mr. Shima. I'm doing everything I'm supposed to do. I'm getting stronger. My latest 5K time on the treadmill is thirty-one minutes. That's not bad for someone recovering from a primary molt, right?" He blinked in his most hopeful, innocent way.

They gave him the fourth-form curriculum. Aster had hacked it, slicing little pockets into the program where she stashed sixth-form uni-prep courses on biosphere, xenosphere, chemistry, physics, maths, and the protocols of research and resource colonies. Exactly the kind of nerdy stuff she loved. While the regular curriculum was running, he could read the more complicated articles in the sidebar. Mostly. He had to re-read a lot, but he had the time.

In fact, he discovered that he could see in the dark. As long as there was some kind of dim light to work with, even as little as the blue and red gleams on the monitor, he could see shape and motion in the eerie grey nightscape of his room. As he got used to this new vision, he could not only read from the faint gleam of the pad but he could make out the presence of people on the other side of the opaque viewing wall because it was only made opaque to human vision. At night there was a single nurse on duty on the other side of the wall, no extra watchers because there was nothing to watch. Now that his primary molt had evidently stabilized, even the day-shift medical personnel came less often, and the nurses didn't pick up the metal food tray the instant he finished. They had other work in their rota, work his transformation had disrupted. Chores they'd neglected that had to get done or they'd get demerits. Their own research to write up to make their personal quotas.

The drone left Meridian. People started to gossip excitedly about the annual advent of a transport from Zenith Colonia. Its in-system arrival was the excuse for the colony's big three-day holiday.

He read harder than he had ever read in his life. Until his head hurt and his eyes leaked slime. But it wasn't enough. It couldn't be enough.

He wrote to Aster, and she agreed.

They would have one chance.

CHAPTER EIGHT

I T TURNED OUT TO BE EASY TO SHIFT THE ROUTINE, TO GET the night nurse used to leaving the food tray for him to pick over as long as he left it on top of the work table beside the door for the morning shift. On the chosen night he pinged Aster via the duodenum, then lay awake, perfectly still, as the hours ticked past. At 0219 he got up as if to use the commode. With the worst acting skills in the universe, borrowed from the dramas he'd seen, he clutched his abdomen and groaned, crawled toward the door, still groaning. No screaming; loud and sudden noises would make the night nurse push the emergency button. Too much groaning and she might push it anyway.

But the nurse did not press the button. The gilded haze of his form left the viewing room. In that brief window of five seconds, Kesh grabbed the tray and positioned himself so the nurse couldn't see him as the door opened. A beam of light probed the empty, rumpled bed.

"Kesh? Are you all right?"

He slammed the tray as hard as he could onto the nurse's head. The man dropped without a sound. The metal smell of human blood leaked into the air. His flesh seemed to vibrate in reaction. He wanted to drop and start sucking and tearing but he didn't. He didn't even have time; he had shoved his leg out to catch the door so it couldn't close. Had he killed the nurse? He could hear shallow breathing—but maybe it was his own.

He didn't have time to check for a pulse, if he could even feel one through the spurs. He slipped out the door with his datapad tucked under his arm. The door shut and latched automatically, lock clicking. As he slid down the corridor as noiselessly as possible, he worked with his teeth at the caps on his fingers until they came free. The translucence of the bone spurs startled him. He tapped them against each other with a satisfying set of clicks. They'd sharpened, becoming more and more like claws.

All of Meridian was laid out in neat sectionals, built by adding on modules. Getting out was easy. Who would dream of breaking out? There was no place for humans in the bush. The colonists were only concerned about things getting in past Meridian's walls.

The thought of seeing Aster again was almost as exciting as escaping being a bug in a lab. She wouldn't be scared of him, would she? He realized he was biting the tips of his claws out of nervousness. With his weird new sharp teeth, he had managed to make his fingers bleed. His blood tasted vile, more like vinegar than nectar.

The hospital doors only locked from the outside, so getting into the main colony was simple. He waved at the security camera before he shoved the door open and stepped out. Some good that footage would do them.

Kesh shivered as he made his way through the shadows. The colony looked alien and lifeless in the dark. Boxy buildings made grey silhouettes against the night sky. Spotlights dotted distant intersections. Once a trash compactor rumbled past, but it didn't have the programming to notice him.

He reached the cargo gate without incident and waited, grateful that the walls cut the wind he could hear knocking together the pods of the trees outside. He wrapped his arms around himself because it was really that cold, not that it helped with him only in a thin hospital gown.

After half an hour of nerve-wracking silence, a short figure appeared, scurrying from corner to corner like she was in a scene from a thriller game, the moody ones in murky gray tones. She was definitely Aster. Even clutching a bundle bigger than her head against her chest, she had the exact same haircut and furtive way of moving. With a start, Kesh realized she hadn't changed at all. Only he had. Maybe he would disgust her now. It wasn't like he wanted to.

She hurried past his shadowed hiding place.

"Aster!" he hissed.

She jolted to a halt and whirled around. "Dammit, you scared me. I mean, is that you?" She narrowed her eyes, squinting into the dark.

He nodded in response, but she couldn't see the subtle movement. "No, it's someone else who waited forty minutes in the cold."

"You're . . . taller than when I saw you last," Aster said, haltingly.

"Also pointier," Kesh mumbled.

"What was that?"

"Never mind. Do you have clothes? I'm freezing." If she

wasn't going to mention obvious physical deformities, neither was he.

"Oh, yeah. Sorry. I hope it fits. I just brought my older brother's stuff." She unrolled the bag and politely turned the other way while he changed as quickly as he could without tearing any of the clothes. He shredded the gown getting it off, although that part was not an accident. The clothes were too large for him and hung off of his arms and over his feet.

"I couldn't get shoes," Aster said. "There might be work boots and jackets in the gate locker."

Kesh ran his hands through his hair again. He could already feel the claws on his feet ripping up the socks. "It doesn't matter. Listen, we need to go. I don't know how soon they'll start looking for me. I had to, uh, hit the night nurse to get out of the room."

"You did what? They're all right, right?"

"Right, right, they're totally all right. You have the code to the gate?"

She hesitated, as if not sure she believed him.

"Aster, I have to go or they'll put me in a bug cage on Earth and I'll die there."

"Dammit." She hugged the collection of stolen datapads to her chest, not moving.

For a horrible dragged-out forever instant, he wondered if he was going to have to hit her over the head to get the datapads. He couldn't do that. Could he? But then she keyed in a code, the door opened, and they slipped into the sealed gatehouse that linked inside to outside.

It had no windows, only solid gates at either end and a ceiling fitted with spray nozzles and defensive slits in case of invasion. She flicked on the light without warning him, and he yelped and covered his eyes. But she screamed and dropped the datapads in a clattering *thunk thunk thunk*.

He filtered the bright fluorescence through his fingers and stared at her as his eyes adapted. "Are you all right?"

Her look of horror was directed at him, her mouth gaped open, eyes so wide they seemed mostly whites.

A nervous, high-pitched laugh bubbled out of Kesh. "It's not that bad, right? I mean, look, I'm still me." He spread his arms and tried to stifle his customary sickly smile. The last thing Aster needed was to get a glimpse of his translucent pointy teeth.

She was breathing hard, like a runner trying to get their breath back.

"I guess so. Yeah. You're, uh, you've got those red patches like . . . and your jaw. I'm sorry, that was so rude of me." She ducked down to gather up the datapads, keeping her gaze down as she kept talking. "They showed pictures of you in class, but it's completely different in person . . ."

"They did what?" The only time he could remember anyone taking pictures of him was during examinations, when he wasn't clothed. He could feel his face starting to heat up. His ability to blush was still human, at least.

Now Aster was blushing, too, more from shame than embarrassment by her scent and the way she wouldn't look at him. Kesh opened one of the lockers meant for outdoor expeditions, thanking the colony again for being so quiet and safe, and pulled on a rain jacket. He grabbed a first aid kit, a field bag, and a pair of boots one size larger than he'd worn before. While he wrestled on the boots, careful with his claws, Aster put the datapads and the first aid kit in the field bag.

Kesh added a knife, a blanket, and one of the winterized coats. Anything he remembered wishing for on his last trip.

"I grabbed a few meal bars. Half a bottle of soap. I couldn't get a comb or change of clothes."

"It's great. Fine. Perfect. I just need to get outside."

When did he start reassuring her?

He caught his reflection in the locker mirror. Hair hanging over his eyes, face split into sections, jagged and translucent teeth and claws, skin insect-spotted, blood from the chew marks on his fingers and at the corner of his mouth. Threads of skin hanging from him like nasty, peeling decay. No wonder Aster had screamed.

He turned back to her. She was holding the field bag and carefully staring at the wall next to him.

"I guess I'm going now," Kesh said. The panic was subsiding, replaced by that familiar hollowness. The fear of being alone.

"Yeah. Hey, uh . . . you look pretty badass, actually. With the red and stuff. It just took me by surprise." She offered him a shy smile. It was almost like having normal Aster back. For this moment, he wasn't alone.

He took the bag from her gingerly, and then when she started to turn away, he hugged her tight and pretended he wasn't crying into her hair like a gigantic baby. She returned the embrace, and he pretended she also wasn't sniffling into his shoulder.

Maybe leaving was a terrible idea after all. Maybe he could find a way to stay.

All at once the alarm went off in a blaring blast of sound, just like the invasion drills. Aster shoved him toward the outer gate. Her face was all red and puffy, and there was a spot of his blood on her jacket. She was going to be in huge trouble.

She punched the code in. The doors ground open.

"Sorry, and thank you," Kesh managed to say before Aster shoved him again and shouted.

"Get out, you idiot!"

He ran.

CHAPTER NINE

I T TOOK THE REST OF THE NIGHT WALKING AWAY FROM Meridian before he started to smell the odor of sansik on some of the trees. It was strongest in gouge marks regularly carved deep into the fibrous meat of the trunks. The sansik were harvesting something, that was for sure, but he wasn't sure if it was sap, the wood itself, or those round, glistening fruits. These sansik had a different scent than Queenie did. Maybe they were from a different hive. Maybe they'd kill him as soon as they saw him. No, that wasn't a helpful thought. He just had to keep moving.

Kesh followed the scent's trail, pretending that he could make out that it was the path Queenie had followed. He kept to the shadows and forged a route through the heaviest growth of vegetation. All too frequently while scanning the dark canopy for buzzing hovercraft, he would trip over a vine or root and stumble, hit his knee or elbow, and ooze a little more of his sludgy blood.

Every time, he felt a little stupider. He wasn't even good at being a wasp.

He wanted to rest, but his whole body ached whether he walked or not, so he kept walking, long past exhaustion.

As dawn lightened the world, he trudged through sticky scrub brush, through tight stands of intertwined thorn trees, through tangle pines bristling on rocky ridges. It had all looked the same from the colony, but in the thick of the rainforest, he was starting to tell the differences even in twilight's gloom: the bulbous purple scrub clustered around the trees, the pink tinges where the fruit got the most light. The sparser patches of undergrowth, as if those areas were the heaviest traveled.

His hearing had changed. He didn't think the sense itself had improved so much as he was just better at listening. When needle-leaves started shaking with a regular vibration, he knew it was the approach of a ground vehicle well before it came into sight. It was easy to make himself small in the dense overgrowth.

Twice that morning, field jeeps drove within sight of his hiding place. Once when he was tucked into a rotten log amid squirming grubs nuzzling his feet through the rips in his socks and boots, and the other time when he was squeezed into a dense grove of thorn trees. The field jacket's fabric repelled thorns as effectively as it repelled wind, which meant he could tug its hood up over his head and not get scratched. The jacket even had a camouflage setting. The hood just smelled of boring old locker dust and slightly heated wiring, like his closet back at the colony, which made his chest ache in its own way. It wasn't that he had been particularly happy growing up, but now he missed the routine of it.

Maybe that was why he didn't pay enough attention when he finally squirmed out of the thorn trees, covered in pulp and dew. A sanguinolent wasp stood an arm's length from him—not his short arms, but its arms, its curled razors. Kesh's breath caught sharply in his chest. It was huge.

The wasp's head was turned away from him, antennae-stubs twitching. At the base of its head, the shell was cracked in like an egg. Something had hit it hard. Dried red fluid crusted the wound, just like human blood. Maybe Queenie had dealt that blow. The wasp smelled hateful. A rage rose in him, worse than the panic. It just stood there, huge, ugly, deadly, in his way.

Everyone just kept getting in his way!

He stepped forward, instead of back. Old needles crackled under his boot.

The wasp snapped around to stare at Kesh. It had five eyes that shone red, red. The sixth had been torn out. It rubbed its mandibles together, working its own leaking fluid into its mouth.

All of his anger evaporated in the dead-eyed, crimson stare of the sanguinolent wasp. He backpedaled, feeling behind him for his pack with the knife in it. For a moment the wasp didn't move, and Kesh prayed he was beneath its notice.

Then it flared its vestigial wings and clattered forward, swaying unsteadily on its feet. The hit on its head must have been serious. It was still twice his size, maybe three times with the crimson wings flared and rattling in a horrific death-song. Kesh stumbled back another step, finally closing his hand around the strap of the pack. He pulled it to his chest and fumbled the cover open.

The wasp found its footing and charged him, mouth open so he could see every jagged spine in its gear-like maw.

Everything else up until this moment had been practice.

This time, he really was going to die.

His hand closed around the knife, and he tripped backward just as the wasp's claws punctured the air where he had been.

Its head swiveled, disoriented, buying him just enough time to yank the knife out of the pack and switch it open.

In his small hand, against the wasp, it looked more like a can opener than a weapon. If he'd had time, or breath, he would have laughed, but in the space of opening the knife, the wasp realized he was below it and stepped onto his leg. Pinning him in the mud.

Kesh threw his arm up between the teeth and his face, with the sudden thought that he wasn't sure if he was more willing to lose his stupid face or his clumsy hand—but instincts won out. The wasp ripped his sleeve, mandibles scraping across Kesh's exoskeleton.

It almost looked taken aback, rearing back to spit out the plastic coat with distaste. Kesh found the knife the right kind of weight in his hand, the wasp's next movement oddly slow as it ducked down to maul him again. His own rotten face, twisted in fear, reflected in its unblinking eyes.

He punched the point of the knife through the wounded eye, the wasp's own weight driving the blade in past the hilt, driving the knife in so deep that his knuckles were swallowed by the socket.

The wasp's weight shifted onto him, crushing him, the mandibles hanging open over his head ready to snap shut. Kesh didn't move.

Neither did the wasp.

His hand felt like it was covered in jelly. The smell of blood mingled with the oppressive musk of the wasp. The scent was disgusting. Infuriating. He wanted to scream, or cry. All he could do was count and force himself to breathe. It was dead, he told himself. It was dead. He was okay.

Eventually, he managed to squirm out from under it, even

with his hand still stuck in the wet shell. Why was it so hard to pull the knife out? He needed it! And why wasn't the wasp bleeding? Was this something they'd covered in school? Physics, maybe . . . suction, or . . . maybe he had to let go of the knife.

Letting go of the handle worked. He pulled his hand out, gagging. Warm fluid gushed out over his wrist; it was purple and somehow smelled *worse* than the rest. Kesh shouted a hoarse, wordless cry, trying to clear his mind, but all he could do was tremble. The wasp's corpse lay contorted on the ground, open wings limp.

Wasn't this what he'd daydreamed of? Winning?

Why was even victory so awful?

Kesh reminded himself to breathe, once, twice, again. Finally, he dug the knife out of the wasp's punctured eye. It came out with a sucking noise and fluid spurted all over his jacket. When he tried to wipe off the fluids that had splattered over him, patches of skin sloughed off his hand.

Gagging, he dug into the pack for anything strong enough to cover that suffocating smell. He tore a strip off the blanket and poured water over it and tied it over his nose and mouth, and that helped some. The blanket smelled like moist protein bar, which was musty and processed, but at least he could think now.

He walked a few steps away and collapsed on the ground. His arm bled, moisture seeping through the jacket and into the cold.

The wasp's body sprawled on the ground face-first in the ferny muck. It seemed duller and smaller in death than it had in life. Even so, there was no way he could carry that thing to the hive, to prove that the fluids smeared all over him weren't a sign of him turning into a wasp but instead that he'd killed one. To prove he was on the sansik's side, not an enemy.

He sat for what seemed like an hour, gathering strength for what he had to do, then got up and searched around the neck for a joint. His fingers found a fleshy seam between the head armor and the body. With a deep breath, he leveraged the knife into the seam and sawed. Two cuts in, the blade hit something hard and the knife scraped and he jumped, hands up. He left the knife lodged in the wasp again, staggered away, and almost puked. He walked in a brisk circle until winter's cold replaced the memory of the grate of blade on bone.

Outside skeleton. Inside skeleton. His and Aster's old surgery game didn't seem like much fun now.

He returned, steadied his breathing, and tried again, harder this time. But the knife wasn't sharp enough or strong enough. Or he wasn't strong enough.

Old lessons crowded back into his mind from xenobiology class. Female wasps were the really dangerous ones because they lived as long as sansik and injected their eggs into their victims, leaving them alive until the egg hatched inside them like he had in his father. Male wasps were dangerous because they killed to eat or for territory, but they only lived long enough to reproduce—one short season.

Was that all he had to look forward to? One short season?

It didn't matter. He was here now. He'd made his choice. He had to go on.

He shoved the knife into the front pocket of the bag and left the wasp's corpse behind.

The next day passed in a blur as he followed the scent trail. Twice, during the morning, he caught the flash of hovercrafts on the horizon and dived into cover. As the day wore on, he saw no one else. Probably they had given up, glad to be rid of the parasite in their midst.

Late in the afternoon, a gleam of purple flashed in the distance, moving in the brush. Sansik! Kesh hollered and ran toward them, then stumbled to a stop. Wait. Wait. He smelled like a wasp. Making noise and charging was wasp behavior.

He started forward again, keeping his steps slower and even. There were six, with maybe more out of sight. They stopped harvesting and watched him approach with their glittering eyes and shiny features devoid of human expression. The wings on their back lifted, ready to warning-rattle.

"Hello?" Kesh said, when he was close enough that he was reasonably certain they could hear him. He kept his arms by his sides. Small. Non-threatening. "I come in peace."

The sansik took a step backward in unison.

"I am a human. I smell like a wasp because one attacked me and I killed it. You, uh, can see the blood's all over me. It's pretty gross. May I speak with a translator? I am trying to find Queenie. She knows me. She knows my smell. I have something for her, something she wants."

The sansik turned all together and walked away, turning their backs. Another rejection. He swore under his breath as the ugly flood of despair rose again. No use in it, no point. Why not just lie down and die?

No.

He'd killed a wasp, however clumsily and badly and because it was already half dead anyway. But he was alive. He pulled the pack up higher on his shoulder and followed.

The sansik didn't seem distressed, and none moved to stop him as he trailed them back to the hive. They never once made a sound, though he thought he could scent varying signals from them even if he didn't know what those signals meant. Maybe, with some practice, he could learn.

They arrived at the lumpy hill-like protrusion of the hive from a direction he didn't recognize, to an entrance he didn't realize was there until a Queenie-colored sansik appeared as if out of nowhere. This sansik stepped between him and the workers, who dropped to all eights and crawled under a netting of ferns and roots one by one.

The sansik stared at Kesh with its bright, blank eyes. Kesh looked back, fighting down both his fear and euphoria. He'd done it, hadn't he? He'd found the hive. The right hive, even. And, while he'd like to sit down before he decided, he was pretty sure he hadn't died yet.

"Let me talk to you before you kill me," Kesh said. "I know you can understand me. I want to talk to Queenie. She's the wasp-killer, right? That's her job? Wasp-killer and translator. We don't really have a job like that in Meridian."

I am Queenie, the sansik said. Her voice had the same grinding growl, but she smelled wrong.

"No, you're not Queenie. I can tell."

A minty scent. Confusion? A broken pattern?

Why does it matter which unit you speak to?

"It matters to me! It just does! Since we talked before! I want to talk to someone I know! I want to talk to Queenie. And she wants to talk to me. I have information about the pinewheat blight."

The sansik stared at him. Or he thought she was staring. It was hard to tell when they never blinked. The late afternoon sunlight played a mottled pattern over the sheen of its carapace. The sansik turned around and vanished, past the net of vegetation, into the tunnel.

CHAPTER TEN

K ESH FOUND A LOG TO SIT ON AND HUGGED HIS PACK. IT would be dark in an hour and a lot colder soon. He was already shivering. Still, if worst came to worst, he could sleep right here and try again in the morning. Plus, he still had that blanket, even with a strip ripped off the corner.

In the silence he heard voices carrying on the wind. At first he was sure he had to be hallucinating because of fear and exhaustion and starvation, but he wasn't starving. He'd had protein bars. Then he realized he could smell the sour, fetid scent of humans.

He stuck the pack into a hollow of the log and crept around the irregular base of the hive until he could overlook the main entrance, hiding himself behind a rocky protuberance and screen of thorn brush. A lander rested on open ground about one hundred meters from the entrance. Of course they'd known he would come here. They knew which hive had brought him back, and where else did he have to go?

Chief Executive Vandelier and Dr. Shima waited at the base of the ramp, looking impatient and bored. Worse, Aster stood with arms crossed between two security guards. He scrambled away, breaking branches, rustling leaves, then stopped himself, panting.

No one shouted after him. They hadn't heard him. They couldn't smell him.

He hurried back to where he'd left his pack. There were three sansik waiting at the log. The scent and the way one of them moved seemed right. Kesh walked up to her, and she let him. He put his hand on her chest and craned up to see. His scraped line marked her armor.

"Queenie!" He hugged her.

Queenie felt surprisingly warm. She just stood there, with his arms half circling her armored waist, and he started crying again because he wanted her to embrace him back as if she cared, but she never would because she was a giant alien bug and he was crazy for wanting affection from a giant bug. Clinically crazy. No wonder the doctors figured he'd make their reputations and raise their aggregation score exponentially. No wonder they wanted to send him back to Earth so everyone could study him, the freak wasp child.

Queenie pressed talons gently on his back so he would release his grip. Her big head and bright eyes loomed over him.

Kesh Ugomi, you have an offer for us.

It took him an eternity to find his voice.

". . . I want to live with you."

If your colony will not tolerate Kesh Ugomi wasp larva, this colony will not tolerate Kesh Ugomi wasp larva.

"I don't want to be tolerated! I want to be a part of the colony. I brought a database. To help with the blight."

One of the other sansik spoke suddenly. *We will not tolerate sanguinolent wasp attempt to propagate within our halls.*

He swallowed, and then it all burst out. "I'm male! See, so I couldn't propagate in your colony if I tried. I can't lay eggs. I'll be dead by next year anyway! I just don't want to be studied and poked, I don't want to be alone, and they'll separate me from everyone I know and send me to Earth and cut me up and I'll never see anyone ever again because they're all lying bastards anyway!"

After a pause, as if they were all waiting to see if he had more to say, Queenie spoke. *Is Kesh Ugomi wasp larva tolerated in your colony?*

"Yes. They didn't kick me out. I ran away. You hear them outside, right? They're going to try to get me back."

Queenie watched him expressionlessly. Queenie was always expressionless. They were all expressionless. He had to convince giant bugs that he was human. Her antennae twitched.

"Kesh is my name. It's not what humans call wasp people, because I'm the only one like me. I'm not really a wasp. I'm human. I have hands like a human, and four limbs like a . . . like a human." He held his hands out, thought about how ridiculous he must look to them, a creature who could not do any of the tasks they needed in their hive. "Also you need me to work the datapads. They're made for human hands like mine."

Queenie said, *Kesh is correct. Meridian hive has come to take Kesh wasp larva back to colony. They do not trade, only take.*

"Yeah, humans fight a lot about territory and scores and who has the most and who doesn't have enough. That's how it always was on Earth. Uh . . . the world that we came from. Out in space. Like . . . from the sky."

She was unimpressed by this revelation. *Extraplanetary origin of Meridian hive is documented.*

"Oh. So . . . I think Executive Vandelier is afraid you're trying to take advantage of Meridian. That you don't want us here and want to push us out. But there's lots of room for everyone here on this planet. Isn't there?"

Territory disputes signal incomplete hive, Queenie said. *Uncivil wasp behavior. Proper colonies share information and territory.*

"Is that what you mean by asking if they tolerate wasp larvae?" He thought about the company and the quotas and the aggregation scores everyone obsessed over. "Yeah, I guess maybe? Huh."

We will consult, Queenie said.

She turned to the other sansik, pressed her head against theirs, and began a series of taps and clicks. To his surprise, Kesh found that he could follow the pattern even if he didn't know what it meant.

He was learning, after all. And he could continue to learn.

Eventually Queenie turned back and knelt to bring her eyes level to his.

Is this Kesh Ugomi larva's first molting? Queenie said. *Clumsy.*

"First . . . what?" He looked at his arms. They were covered by the coat. "No, this is a coat."

Queenie flared her wings and reached for him. Kesh shrank back.

Remove or . . . Queenie stopped, tilted her head, then made a motion with one talon like she was scraping something off her shell. *Fungus. Remove before we speak to Executive.*

"Humans don't do this normally," Kesh said. "Did I do something wrong? Am I going to get an infection?"

She clasped his face in a claw. Now here it came. Her claws would tear through his cheek and kill him for bringing more fungus into her hive. At least it would be fast.

Instead she caught his shedding skin with the ridges on her forearms. She . . . meant to groom him.

"Wait." He stripped off his clothes. With the coat off he really was peeling everywhere, skin hanging like dried out threads. Gross. "Okay. So fungus can get under here when you molt?"

Again she caught at his skin.

Yes. Damp. Fragile, she said, pausing. *Careful.*

She carefully tugged at the shreds. Her own dry sansik smell cloaked the odor of wasp. He bit his lip and closed his eyes until Queenie was done scraping the discard off of him.

Now you have shed being a larva. Queenie straightened up and tilted her head to regard him.

He opened his eyes and examined his arms, legs, torso. The cleaning had revealed the crimson, black, and purple of his carapace under the dull human skin. It lay around him, a grey wrapper over his true vibrancy. His shell glistened.

"What am I now? An adult?" That sounded cool. And living with the sansik, he wouldn't have to do taxes or worry about aggregation scores. Not that he would have made it that far anyway.

No. You are Kesh. We will speak to the Executive.

She hooked the pack out of his hands and, with the others, walked away around the hive. He pulled on undergarments and trousers, but they didn't wait for him, so he bundled up the torn-up boots, shirt, and coat and ran after them. They used a path he hadn't noticed before, one that wove easily between clusters of brush and mounds of heaped dirt and rock whose shapes no longer seemed random but designed. His bare feet felt soft but sturdy, human feet with little claws and a weird texture. Tender but strong.

He scanned the sky, listening to the clack of branches, sniffing the heavy but not unpleasant odor of the sansik all around him. The sunset was remarkably beautiful, cool reds and long yellows. The people from Earth complained that Meridian wasn't beautiful the way Earth was, but now that he had started paying attention, it wasn't so bad.

It wasn't so bad until he had to walk out onto the flat ground into full view of the lander. Seeing him, Vandelier grimaced with disgust. Dr. Shima gasped with a grin of delight, like he'd won a prize. Aster clenched her jaw, looking stormy and mad. But when he tried to catch her eye, she looked away, like she was disgusted too.

His arms were uncovered. His skin looked weird, spiky, and broken at his joints, but at least it was mostly human-colored. Mostly human-shaped. It meant he wasn't really a wasp, right? He was still a person. He had a right to live as he wished, even if it was to be only one short season.

Vandelier stared at him with cold black eyes. Well, they were really brown, but from this distance and in the grey winter twilight, they may as well have been black.

"Kesh Ugomi. So you are alive."

"Sorry to disappoint you," Kesh said. When he stared back at Vandelier, she looked away. He stood a little straighter. Let her be nervous. He probably looked terrifying with his claws and pointy carapace. That was cool.

Vandelier's lips pinched with distaste. She addressed Queenie instead. "Return Kesh Ugomi to us—"

"I'm not going back," Kesh said.

Vandelier gave him a look that at best was scorn and more

likely the same unfiltered look of hatred the kids at school used to give him right before they'd dump juice over his head. But she was the head of the colony. She wasn't supposed to act like a bullying kid.

"Aster, don't you have something to say to Kesh?"

Aster was still stuck between the two guards, all scrunched up like she was hoping to break and run.

Without looking at him, she spoke in a quick-patter monotone like a memorized speech. "Kesh, you have to come back. No one can take care of you out here. It will be better for the colony because we will get a great aggregation score. Don't you want to help everyone who helped keep you alive? Don't you want to see Earth? Like, wouldn't that be the coolest thing? I hope to go to Earth someday too, and maybe I can see you there as we enjoy Earth together."

He twitched his nose. She smelled sour with nervousness but also tangy, almost lemony, like she was about to bust up laughing at one of the dumb jokes she and he would share. In fact, this was obviously a joke because Aster's parents had signed a thirty-year contract to the company, one that had tied Aster and her brother into the contract too. She complained all the time about Earth's greedy corporate talons and how she was going to make it better for colonists somehow, some way.

"If you won't listen to me, you should listen to your friend," said Vandelier with an emphasis on *friend* as if she knew perfectly well Kesh only had one friend. "I don't think you understand the situation fully. If you do not return to the colony with us now, you are going to die. We can help you."

Hearing the words out loud made him weak in the knees. He didn't want to be a wasp. What if they really could help him? "Can you make me human again?" he asked, hating the pathetic whine of his voice. "I just want to go back to when I was human."

"You were never human," said Vandelier.

A flare of wasp-fierce anger reddened his gaze. "Well, I guess you'd know because you were born a jackass."

Aster snorted and then clapped a hand over her mouth and coughed like she'd just sucked in a lungful of fungus and dirt.

Vandelier flushed red. "Take Aster back into the lander. I told you there was no reason to bring her," she added to Dr. Shima.

"No, no, I said I'd convince Kesh and I will," Aster said, twisting away from the guards. She put both hands up to fend them off. The guards looked at each other—and with that look he realized they were the same pair who'd brought him into the airlock—and took a step back like they did not want to be involved and were sorry they'd come at all. Good. Let them be sorry.

"Let Aster be," said Dr. Shima. "We wouldn't know he'd come here if she hadn't told us."

Aster *had* told them! But why help him escape and then rat him out? It didn't make sense. Not unless there was something else going on, something else Aster had planned. She was always good at strategy. Maybe there was something he didn't know. He squinted at Aster, trying to read her mind.

Vandelier again addressed Queenie. "Return Kesh Ugomi to us along with the datapads he stole. He has no right to that information and neither do you."

Queenie said, *Information contained for the use of only one colony is valueless.*

"Yet you've stolen our child and our information," Vandelier said, completely without irony. "So it has value to you."

"The sansik didn't steal anything." Kesh puffed up his chest, hoping he looked like some badass delinquent punk-wasp hybrid. "I left Meridian to come live with the sansik. That's my right. I get to make that choice because I molted and that makes me an adult. You can't boss me around anymore."

"You *molted* and that makes you an adult?" Vandelier wrinkled her nose.

"Yeah! That's what Queenie said." He could feel his face flush. "Am I a human or not? Actually, it doesn't matter, does it? I'm a *person* either way, so I have a right to my own life!"

"You have *rights* because of Meridian. You have a duty to Meridian," said Vandelier. "Your care and upkeep has cost the colony, so you owe a significant debt. I'm calling in that debt. If you don't return, you'll be prosecuted as a thief."

Kesh may not leave, Queenie said. *We require the information he brought to us. Kesh has no value to us. We will not trade for him again.*

"I hope you don't mean 'no value,'" Kesh said, trying to choke down a bubble of nervous laughter. "I really hope you mean 'invaluable.'"

There was an awkward pause.

There is no value we will exchange Kesh for, Queenie said. She leveled her gaze at Vandelier in a way that wasn't violent, or threatening as humans judged threat, but which was implacable and unmovable.

The sansik were going to keep him. It was like a seed of hope bursting into full sparkling bloom in his heart.

"Are you going to tell them, or should I?" asked Vandelier, of Dr. Shima. She didn't wait for Dr. Shima's answer. She was too eager to drop the bomb. "You can't keep Kesh Ugomi because Kesh Ugomi is female. You sansik can't allow a female sanguinolent wasp into your hive, can you?"

"What?" Kesh's voice pitched up in anger. Fear. "You're lying."

"I'm not lying. Ask Dr. Shima."

Dr. Shima sighed with his sad sorry eyes, the ones brightened by excitement at his good luck in being present for the first known alien-human hybrid. This would make his career. "It's true, Kesh. You're not a male wasp. You're a female."

The other sansik clicked with arrhythmic consternation and rapidly retreated. Queenie took several steps away.

"Checkmate." Vandelier's smile was a giant gloating sun. "You're a danger to everyone, Kesh. You're lucky Shima argued the others out of just mercy killing you. You might live for decades, losing your identity to your nasty little wasp instincts, piece by piece."

He croaked out, "This is a joke, right? Aster, tell me it's a joke?"

Aster sucked in a tight breath. He couldn't read her face; maybe he could never read human expressions again. But she smelled like honey.

Walking slowly, bravely, toward Queenie, she started talking in a loud voice. "You are a female wasp, Kesh. But they extracted your egg sac—"

"Shut your mouth!" snapped Vandelier, but the executive still hung back, too afraid of the sansik to go after Aster.

Aster addressed Queenie directly. "My parents told me that Dr. Shima harvested the egg sac days ago, so I checked after Kesh left. Kesh doesn't have any eggs. He can't make anyone a parasite. The sansik are safe. Not that our scientists did it for the sansik's sake. They only did it to trade wasp eggs to corporate for a higher aggregation score. But they also had to make sure he never broke out and put an egg in another human. A female wasp would be a threat to us humans too, obviously. That's how his dad died."

Vandelier was shouting at the guards, who did not move to go after Aster or get any closer to the sansik.

Aster said, "Do you understand what I'm saying, Chief Executive Sansik? Kesh has no egg sac. He won't grow another one. He is no threat to your hive."

I listen, said Queenie.

Aster reached Kesh, grabbed his undershirt, and pulled it up to reveal the abdominal scar. "This is the surgery where they took it out. There are scans from the surgery on this clip, which I'm giving to Kesh now"—she slid a wafer drive into his trouser pocket—"so you can see for yourself that he's safe."

Dr. Shima started to laugh.

Vandelier snarled, "You'll pay for this, Aster Tiu—"

"Oh, shut up," said Dr. Shima. "We still have the data and a living subject."

Queenie prodded the scar on Kesh's abdomen. She clicked her teeth and pressed her mandibles against his face as if taking in his wasp scent. Or as if she would rip off his head for sure this time.

Aster whispered, "Kesh?"

"It's okay," he whispered back.

Queenie let him go. She turned toward the other humans. *We will not exchange Kesh. Negotiations have been concluded. You may now depart.*

And they did. Vandelier snarling, Shima beaming his strange smile, and the escort of guards all boarded the hovercraft's extended ramp.

Aster hugged him. In a low voice she said, "I came because I knew Vandelier would pull this trick. I know it sucks, but it's better than going to Earth, right?"

Kesh nodded.

"I'll figure out a way to visit," she said.

He rested his head against her hair. She still smelled weird—oily—but in a nice, friendly way. "I know you will. When you do, can you, uh . . . bring more blankets?"

"Blankets?"

"It's been cold!"

Aster laughed.

The lander's engines rotored on, blowing dust. Aster let go of Kesh and ran to the ramp. Even with him here, she wasn't going to chance being left behind with the sansik.

But she'd promised to return, and that was something to look forward to.

CHAPTER ELEVEN

KESH WOKE UP AT DAWN CURLED UP IN A BLANKET IN Queenie's lap. Carefully, he raised his head so as not to startle her.

Queenie was already awake, of course. He didn't think he'd ever seen her sleeping. He thought with a snort that even for an emotionless bug monster tasked to kill creatures like him, she was paying better attention to him than any of Meridian's adults ever had.

Queenie tilted her head. It seemed she was trying to decide if he was awake. Kesh stretched. His limbs popped and he winced.

"Good morning. I hope I'm not keeping you from your duties."

Kesh is my priority.

Queenie lumbered to her feet, put a claw gently on his shoulder, and steered him out of the little translucent cell-like room down a winding corridor and into a cavern. Here lay an oily pool mixed with bits and pieces like threads and scales. Other

sansik were here scraping themselves. A molting room, maybe like the gym showers back home.

Afterward she led him to a large room full of workers. All simultaneously paused in their chores when Queenie and Kesh entered the room. It was probably the largest room he'd seen yet, domed, warm and dry. Large-stalked plants were growing in it, much chewed-on. The leaves and stems teemed with tiny, crawling life that the workers were shaking off into waxy, hollow shells. They raised their heads in unison and fixed Kesh with a blank stare. He stepped back, discomfited by the wall of unblinking eyes.

Eat, Queenie said. Her scent changed, harsher, smokier. For a moment he had a vision of the sansik eating him, but no—she meant *he* should eat. After a moment, maybe satisfied that they weren't needed for anything, the workers turned back to tending the plants.

Kesh stepped forward at Queenie's continued prodding, put a hand on one of the plants, and looked back at Queenie. She didn't move or offer any further instruction. When he looked back at the plant, tiny bugs had crawled onto his hand. All over his hand. Kesh shrieked, yanked his hand back, and tried to shake off the bugs.

Queenie took one of the waxy shells from a worker, grabbed Kesh's hand, and put it in the shell, which was already half full of crawly things and plant detritus. Kesh made a strangled noise and closed his eyes, which was worse, because he could feel the bugs squirming their way up toward his sleeve. Queenie's grip was not gentle, and the ridges in her claws were cutting into the ridges in his claws.

Good for growing, Queenie said. *Harden shell.*

She was treating him like a young sansik. She wanted him

to be healthy. He could give it a shot, for her. He took a handful and tried to ignore how they squirmed down his throat when he swallowed.

Satisfied he'd understood, she led him onward. It was almost like a facility tour, Kesh decided. Welcome, new sansik!

The next stop was an even larger room, oval-shaped, and lined with the glowing moss. It only had two entrances, one at each end. A trench with a stream in it ran through them. It was the most pleasant-smelling chamber so far, almost flowery, and definitely warm. Queenie sat him at one end.

Teach, she said.

"To who?" Kesh asked, startled. He was trying to brush the last skittering vestiges of breakfast out of his clothes.

Teach I, Queenie said. She settled down in front of him like a gigantic iron preschooler.

"I need the datapads," Kesh said. Fear suddenly constricted his chest. Surely they wouldn't decide he was useless just because he didn't have the information they needed memorized. Queenie lowered her head for a moment.

When she raised it, she said, *Where are the datapads?*

"In my bag. Where I slept."

Queenie stood again, and leaned over Kesh. *Kesh will stay here,* she said, and clicked her mandibles together.

"Yeah. I'll stay right here."

She left him alone in the room. It darkened at her exit. He was almost tempted to go exploring, but there was no doubt that she would be able to tell that he'd been moving around. He waited, long enough in the silence that a fresh wave of loneliness and despair washed through him. He buried his face in his hands, trying not to hyperventilate. What had he been thinking? That he would make carnivorous alien insect friends?

Would it have been better to accept his fate as a freak, a parasite, and go to Earth?

The sound of moss crushing underfoot broke up his frantic thoughts. The flowery scent grew stronger after each sound. Kesh uncovered his eyes, expecting to see Queenie with his pack clutched comically in an oversized set of claws.

Other sansik filed into the cave, of all colors and sizes.

"Uh . . . hello?" he said. "Queenie . . . um, my translator said that I could sit here. I'm not interrupting anything, am I?"

No answer. More sansik were crowding in. Some of them settled into sitting positions, in a rough semicircle around him.

Kesh put his hands on his legs and sat up straight to stare back at them, trying to make himself look bigger but not threatening. The sansik shifted around. Kesh craned his neck to see Queenie shouldering her way back in, his bag resting on her shoulder. When she reached the front, she lowered the pack onto his head carefully.

Kesh settled the bag on his lap and sorted the datapads out of the mess of food crumbs and even the dried remains of mud. Aster had wrapped the pads in a sealed bag so they were clean, and he'd heard that field pads were made to be waterproof and rough-conditions-ready anyway.

He set the bag to one side and switched the datapad on.

Blank.

Is this enough preparation? Queenie said, crushing moss under her as she settled next to him.

Kesh bit his lip. "Yes," he lied, and fiddled with the switch. The datapad made a halfhearted beep and began to boot up. The screen was dim but legible. It had a month's worth of battery, if he didn't play too many games on it. He breathed a sigh of relief as quietly as possible and added a charger to the mental list of things he wanted to ask Aster for.

The rapt attention of the sansik was a strange thing to get used to, but for the first time Kesh felt like he was sharing something that made a difference. He'd been slow at learning, but maybe he could remember how that felt and become the kind of patient teacher that he'd always wished for.

He looked up and smiled, and then remembered that teeth-baring was probably threatening, and coughed and covered his mouth. "So . . . what do you guys want to hear about first?"

Pinewheat, Queenie said.

He skimmed the list, using his knuckle instead of the claws to navigate the display. It was funny, because all of the titles were exactly the kind of thing he hated about school. Yet it was easier to concentrate with an iron-shelled alien tapping and clicking along with him, using the ground as her pad. He had her attention.

"Let's see, there's . . . 'Proposal for Modified Irrigation Systems for Pinewheat to Restrict Spread of Blue Blight—'"

The moment he said *blight* there came a collective rustling in the crowd.

That one, Queenie said.

Kesh cleared his throat, and began to read the text aloud.

—END—

ACKNOWLEDGEMENTS

IT WAS A STRANGE, HARD ROAD TO COMPLETING THIS NOVELLA, and I'm not sure how to properly thank all involved. First of all I'd like to thank my mom, Alis Rasmussen, who helped me restructure the work into the shape it takes here. A much more uplifting and satisfying end than I'd originally planned. I'd also like to thank my wife, Melanie Ujimori, my rock, who supports me through fair weather and foul. Thanks as well to a particular box of rats—you know who you are—and especially to Jay Castellanos, Zoey Hogan, and Veles Svitlychny, who have repeatedly assured me that I am, in fact, a genius, and to OCBZ, who put up with a lot of funny business over this last decade and many, many bugs. And lastly, a hearty thanks to Nick Mamatas, who introduced me to Vernacular Books, without whom this story would not be in your hands now.

Writing is lonely work. Thank you for coming on these odd journeys alongside me.

CPSIA information can be obtained
at www.ICGtesting.com
Printed in the USA
BVHW030751020322
630339BV00001B/39